SAMANTHA SAVAGE
BEAST HUNTRESS

Blood Fangs

Samantha Savage
Beast Huntress

Episode II

By R.C. Farrington
Illustrated by Jason Farrington

ISBN-10: 1927750180
ISBN-13: 9781927750186

www.bermudaspinners.com

Wonderful People
who contributed to this book:

Jason Farrington has created outstanding graphic designs for this novel. www.gorilladesignstudio.net

Rod Ferguson of Bermuda and Pat Farrington of the United States have made contributions of their time and thoughts to help make this novel possible.

I would also like to extend a special thank you to Delta Air Lines for all the smooth trips and outstanding flight crews on my many flights to and from Bermuda. Because of this I was able to write a large portion of this novel while in the air with Delta.

DEDICATION

I would like to dedicate this book to my readers and fans. Without the avid readers in Bermuda and the tourists who visit Bermuda, these novels would not have been possible. Their enthusiasm and positive response have helped keep my creative imagination going over the years. Not to mention the historic, cultural, and scenic settings that only Bermuda has to offer as an inspiration. There is no doubt why other writers over the years, including Mark Twain, found Bermuda one of the most beautiful and inspirational places on earth.

INTRODUCTION

Bermuda is the most beautiful place on earth, and whoever reads this novel should take at least one week out of his/her busy life to visit one of the most incredible places on the earth. There you will find soft, pristine turquoise-colored waves gently rolling up on the pink beaches. You will also find breathtaking the myriad combinations of arbors, shrubs, vines, and flowers that reflect all the colors of the rainbow. Then, when you consider the historic forts, the village of St. George's, and the most picturesque golf courses in the world...yes, Bermuda is truly an island paradise.

CHAPTERS:

Blood Fangs

SAMANTHA SAVAGE
BEAST HUNTRESS

CHAPTER 1

Another Day
in Paradise

ANOTHER DAY
IN PARADISE

Samantha Savage had become a loner, but this was not always the case. A beautiful and brilliant young woman with blonde hair, sea-blue eyes, and a height of just over six feet made it hard for her to go unnoticed. In her late twenties with a master's degree in criminology, Sam had always been interested in law enforcement, but she never felt comfortable joining the Bermuda Police Department as her father had done. She knew she would always live among the shadows of her famous father, Inspector Ian Savage, who had been a local police inspector for the St. George's branch of the Bermuda Police Force. Inspector Savage was one of the most decorated police officers in the history of the Bermuda Police Department. Sam had instead chosen to become a private investigator with her own detective firm, Triangle Detective Agency. Along with four friends, she had been a very successful treasure hunter in her younger days, and she was now one of the wealthiest women in Bermuda.

This morning, just like every morning, she was walking along a small beach looking out over the sun-glistening water. She used to reminisce about her friends and family and how she missed them, but those days were over now. She had chosen self-isolation some time ago. In fact, she had no idea how long she had been living on this beautiful deserted island. Until she became comfortable in her own skin and could understand what she had become, she would remain in self-isolation. She did not fear for her own life, but for the lives of others who might come in contact with her.

As she neared the end of the beach, she started to jog, though her intent was not to run but to leap. She built up speed and then leaped over fifty feet into the air, clearing the palm trees. She landed in a small clearing and leaped again. This time she landed in a palm tree and began swinging and leaping from palm tree to palm tree. No, she did not think for a moment she was Tarzan, but she was sure she could outmaneuver him in any jungle. Shortly after that, Sam came across her favorite boulder, which was two feet in diameter and weighed over five hundred pounds. She walked over to it, bent down, picked it up, and gave it a toss. The boulder landed about twenty yards away. She never tried to throw it too far because she wanted to keep the boulder in her morning exercise pathway.

After the boulder exercise, she continued on her morning obstacle course. She was beginning to feel good about her powers, but she still feared her dark side. The daylight hours were fine for her; however, the night was a whole different story. Not only was she still haunted by the events that drove her to this tiny island, but she could also feel physical changes in her body.

Later that night as she lay in the darkness of her hut, she found herself once again drifting into her past. That final night before her transformation she vividly remembered being tied up in the back of a speeding van. At a very high speed, the van had crashed through a police car roadblock causing flames and explosions all around her. A short time later she found herself at the Unfinished Cathedral in the village of St. George's, Bermuda. From this point on, the events of that night were fuzzy. She remembered Zuka, a vampire who was her captor, demanding the key to the gateway for the Bermuda Triangle. Yes, vampires and the Bermuda Triangle do exist. Sam had fought off the vampire until he bit her, sinking his fangs deep into her neck. Later when she was regaining consciousness, she found herself being teleported with the vampire into the Bermuda Triangle. In all the chaos of the teleportation she remembered being bitten again by the vampire. The rest of her memories had long since been blocked out. All she could remember now was that she had woken up on a beach in the Bermuda Triangle and found the strength to kill the vampire. Sam had never seen a vampire since, but she assumed someday that might change.

During the twilight hours, some of what she recognized as her vampire attributes took shape. Her two upper canine teeth grew ever so slightly and very sharp. Others would probably never even notice this occurrence, but Sam feared that if she were around humans she might acquire the taste for blood. Although she had never felt the urge, she hadn't seen a human being since arriving back in the Bermuda Triangle.

The vampire that bit her was a hybrid vampire who was never bitten by a vampire beast, but was infected by a diseased vampire bat from the Congo jungle. These vampires developed the same sonar abilities that the bats have, enabling them to sense moving objects in the blackness of the night. Sam also had acquired this ability as well as regeneration healing. If she was cut or wounded in the daylight hours, the wounds were like any other human's, but once the darkness of the night took over, her wounds healed almost instantly.

When angered, her beautiful sea-blue eyes turned blood red and then coal black. She knew that she must be in complete control of her dark side if she ever hoped to return home.

Her home now was in the Bermuda Triangle, which was in another dimension in time. Some might describe it as a "Twilight Zone," or even "Never Land." The apexes of the triangle were Bermuda; Miami, Florida; and San Juan, Puerto Rico. From whichever gateway you entered the triangle, you would find yourself close to parallel to the same space you had left before you went into the Triangle. So if you entered the Triangle in the Atlantic Ocean, you would still find yourself in the Atlantic Ocean, except in a different dimension. It might take you days or weeks to realize that you had been transported. The only clues that you would have that you are here are that compasses would just spin around in circles and guidance and communication equipment would no longer function. You would be confined to the defined area of the Triangle and would just find yourself going around in circles. If you entered the Triangle on a landmass, such as Bermuda, you would still be in Bermuda although you might think you were in a distant paradise. The island remained in the same pristine state it was in over five hundred years ago, before anyone ever stepped foot on it. The wild hogs were still rutting on the island and you might notice that there were other extinct animals, birds, plants, and fish to be found.

The only hope of returning to the dimension from which you came would be to find the same gateway back. Sam, having teleported to and from the Bermuda Triangle over the years, possessed the knowledge and the gateway key to do so. The balance of nature in the Triangle was simple. The existing life in the Triangle evolves and reproduces just like our parallel world; however, if you are a species from another dimension, you enter it sterile. Thus, you can exist in the Triangle but you cannot populate it. While it is a Never Land in which you will remain the same age as when you entered, you can die there since you can be injured or killed just like anyone in our dimension. You just won't age or get any of the diseases of our world. While time stands still in the Triangle, it marches on in our dimension. So if you ever were to find a way to return from the Triangle, you would not re-enter in your time in history, but at the time that had lapsed while you were gone. There are few humans alive in the Triangle today. Most people enter the Triangle from airplanes and ships through temporary gateways in the middle of the Triangle, which is in the Atlantic Ocean. Most planes run out of fuel before finding any landmass and crash in the ocean, leaving the occupants to drown. Most ships usually enter the Triangle through a raging storm or hurricane and are severely damaged on their arrival. They might sink soon after their arrival, or even worse, because they cannot find a landmass without a sense of direction, the sailors and passengers may simply starve to death or die of thirst. This leaves many unmanned ghost ships floating around the waters of the Triangle.

The Triangle is truly a paradise when left alone; however, at times when evil outsiders enter the dimension, the paradise is spoiled. As in our world, Mother Nature is normally able to maintain a reasonable natural balance. In recent times (the past three hundred years), due to an overwhelming invasion of evil beings entering the Triangle, the natural balance of paradise has been changed.

Sam fell asleep each night knowing the next day would be just another day in paradise.

Blood Farms

SAMANTHA SAVAGE
BEAST HUNTRESS

CHAPTER 2

The Ghost Ship

THE GHOST SHIP

Late one afternoon just before dusk, Sam heard a cannon being fired from somewhere in the Great Sound. She ran in the direction of the sound. After a couple of leaps, she made it to the shore. To her amazement, she saw a three-hundred-year-old ghost ship in pursuit of a small sail-tattered yacht. The yacht was heading for what would have been known as Hamilton Harbour. While she watched, the ghost ship fired another cannon volley at the yacht. One cannon ball clipped the starboard side of the yacht. She could now see two men and a woman running around the deck. It was clear to Sam that these people were in a life-threatening position. From Sam's vantage point on what would have been Long Island, she would have to row across the sound in her small punt to help the occupants on the yacht. By the time she launched her punt and began rowing at a very high speed toward Hamilton Harbour, it was dark. As she drew closer to the ghost ship, it was apparent to her that the pirates on the ghost ship had caught up to the yacht. The yacht had been run aground, and the ghost ship had anchored just off shore. There was activity aboard the ghost ship although the shore was quiet. Sam was now within twenty yards of the ghost ship, and she did not want to row the punt any closer so she decided to leap to the centre mast of the ship. That way she could oversee the entire deck at once. With one massive leap, Sam jettisoned herself over fifty feet into the air. She misjudged her leap slightly and on her way down she was just able to grab one of the mast ropes over the crow's nest. Luckily for her, no one was in the crow's nest on lookout. From her perch, she saw the three captives on the deck. One was already dead, surrounded by a pool of blood. The second male was tied to a barrel and was being used for sword practice. The young woman was hanging by ropes from the yardarm. The crew of ten looked like pirates who had been in the Triangle for hundreds of years, but one member of the crew was dressed in more modern clothing. Sam sensed something strange about him, and then it came to her—he was not a human, but a blood beast. Yes, a vampire. Sam tried to keep her composure, but in seconds her eyes went to blood red to black as the night. A moment later as she leaped for the deck, the vampire attacked the young woman. He bit into her neck, spraying blood in all directions.

Sam landed on the back of one pirate and quickly snapped his neck, killing him instantly and catching his sword before it hit the ground. With the sword in hand, she swung by a mast rope and decapitated the next pirate. She quickly picked up his sword and threw it as hard as she could at the vampire. The sword struck the vampire in the chest with powerful force, sending him flying through the air and pinning him to the cabin wall. He struggled to free himself, but it was useless. In the next few minutes, Sam stabbed or shot the rest of the pirates. She then went to the three captives, but it was too late: they were already dead.

Sam walked over to the vampire, who was still hanging on the wall like a slab of meat and shoved her other sword deep into his midsection, twisting it back and forth. She then said, "You bloodsucking bastard, how did you get here?"

The vampire screamed and hissed at Sam, showing his fangs. He replied, "You're a vampire like me. Let me down and share the bounty, my dear."

Sam twisted the sword more and said, "I'm not a vampire, you beast."

In a great deal of pain, the vampire said, "Your black eyes and canines say differently."

10

Sam snapped back, "I want some answers fast, or you'll be a dead vampire."

The vampire laughed, but he knew he was in trouble. He replied, "I'm already dead, but what is it you want to know?"

Sam moved closer to him, gripping the sword tighter. "What are you doing here, and where did you come from?"

The vampire tried to brush off the pain and said, "My clan found a portal to this lost world, and I've been sent here to access its future for us."

Sam replied, "There's no future here for you. Now where are you from?"

The vampire smiled and said, "It doesn't matter. It's a one-way portal to this world. We can see in and pass through, but we cannot return, except for our master. My clan already knows you exist."

Sam grabbed him, squeezing the cheeks on his face and said, "So tell me anyway. Where the bloody hell are you from?"

The vampire replied, "All right, bitch, I'm from New Orleans."

Sam banged the vampire's head against the cabin wall and said, "Thanks, asshole!" She backed up and started to walk away. "I'm not going to kill you. I'm not going to kill you." A second later her eyes turned jet black. She abruptly turned around facing the vampire and ripped out a hunting knife from her boot as she yelled, "The hell I'm not!" She threw the knife, piercing the vampire's chest and heart. The vampire let out a scream and went limp. The undead vampire was now dead by Sam's standards. She walked away and leaned over the ship's gunwale, gazing out over the Great Sound. She now knew the vampires were not just from the past, but they lived in the present. She would dedicate her life to going back to her world and hunting these blood beasts down to eradicate them from the face of the earth.

Before Sam left the ghost ship, she broke open the black powder kegs in the ship's powder room. Just as she was going to leap from the ship, she threw a torch into the room. As soon as she leaped for shore, the black powder ignited and sent a massive ball of flames over one hundred feet into the air.

The old ship blew up into a million pieces. Sam watched the fireworks from the shoreline.

As Sam walked away from the burning wreckage, she knew she had to leave the Bermuda Triangle soon and track down these blood beasts. The quest would begin in New Orleans, but first she would have to go home and make peace with her old friends.

Blood Fangs

SAMANTHA SAVAGE
BEAST HUNTRESS

CHAPTER 3

The Goodbye

THE GOODBYE

Sam had finally come to terms with herself. It was time to go back home and make things right. Not knowing if she was ever going to return to the Bermuda Triangle, she elected to burn her hut and all her belongings. She would leave with the clothes on her back, the Tucker Cross, and nothing else. As she rowed across the Great Sound, she stopped for a minute and looked back at Long Island. The smoke from the fire dominated the sky. The pause was only brief. Sam wanted to make it to the Shark Hole gateway by sunset, if possible. Hours later, Sam finally made it to Shark Hole. She could have made it in a third of the time by leaping, but knowing she would not be back for years or maybe never, she wanted to enjoy her long, quiet hike through the jungle.

Shark Hole was the only two-way gateway into and out of the Bermuda Triangle that she knew of. All the other gateways were either one way or random ones created by certain storm conditions. Years ago she and her friends had left the key to the gateway with the Pilgrims, a small group of Bermuda Triangle survivors who lived in a village they built in the St. George's area in the Triangle. Because the key to the gateway was also the most sought after treasure relic ever found in the western hemisphere, it was best to keep the Tucker Cross in the Bermuda Triangle. The artifact was an incredibly large solid gold cross with seven marble-size green emeralds embedded in it. It was named the Tucker Cross after the treasure hunter Teddy Tucker who recovered it from a sunken shipwreck, the *San Pedro*, a Spanish galleon sunk off the reefs off Bermuda in 1595. The cross was later stolen and stayed missing for years until Sam and her friends found it in Convict Bay in Bermuda. The seven emeralds appear to draw energy from the lighting strikes of intense storms, which becomes the source of power to open the gateways.

Sam made her way down the embankment to a huge fallen rock where she could jump into Harrington Sound. Once in the water, she swam toward the Shark Hole entrance. Inside the cave, Sam aimed the Tucker Cross deep into the interior, and with her own internal power she was able to ignite the cross. Within seconds, the fireworks display kicked in. Green lights began emanating from the entrance while lightning began to strike at the cave. In seconds, the gateway opened wide with the green explosions going on in the cave, but it was next to impossible for Sam to see through to the other side. She could now see that the gateway was wide open. As she passed through the gateway entering the Triangle, a huge explosion was created on the Bermuda Triangle side of the gateway. In a split second, Sam was gone from the Bermuda Triangle. All she could see was a bright green massive object blasting out of the gateway in front of her. The blast was so massive Sam shot out the other side of Shark Hole like a rocket. All she could think about was what a rush it was as she flew through the air. Who would want to leap when you could fly? Her ride ended as quickly as it began. She hit the water at over fifty miles an hour and went head over heels, hydroplaning on the surface of the water. Finally, she came to a stop. It took a minute for her to get her bearings back. Although it was now dark, her sonar senses were quick to guide her back to the shore. Once ashore, Sam sat down on the rocks as the reality sat in. She was finally home but with no idea how long she had been away.

Not far from her, concealed in the dark shadows, a blood beast's head was just breaking the water line in Harrington Sound. The vampire had been tracking Sam since sunset. He had leaped into Shark Hole just as Sam was being drawn into the portal. Sam was so distracted that her sonar senses never picked up the dark intruder. Once Sam had made it to shore, the blood beast swam to a spot on the shore about one hundred yards from her. He quickly left the shoreline and disappeared into the bushes.

Meanwhile, Sam made her way up the hill to Harrington Sound Road. She decided to walk in the direction of St. George's in hopes that someone would give her a lift. Unbeknownst to her, she walked right by the spot where the blood beast was hiding in the bushes watching her. She did pick up a sense of something, but the thick bushes along the road blocked out her sonar. She didn't mind the long walk as it felt good to be home, but she was anxious to find out how long she had been gone and wanted to see her father and friends.

About two miles down the road a taxi pulled over. The driver stuck his head out the window and said, "Honey, it's dark. Do you want a ride?"

Sam replied, "That would be great, but my money is at my office in St. George's. Would you trust me?"

The driver smiled and said, "Hop in, my dear. I trust you."

Sam smiled back and said, "Thank you." She then climbed into the back seat of the van and the taxi drove off. As they drove along, she started having flashbacks about her last van ride to St. George's. Between the crash with the police cars and the vampire bite, she wished she could block those events from her mind.

She desperately wanted to ask the van driver the date, but she couldn't figure out how to without making the taxi driver think she was crazy. Finally, she said, "Sir, do you happen to have today's newspaper?"

The taxi driver replied, "Yes, I just finished reading it before I picked you up. You can take it." He reached back and handed Sam the paper.

Sam replied, "Thanks." She quickly looked for the date at the top of the paper. To her absolute surprise, she had only been gone eight months. In a way, that was a relief. She sat back in the van and read through the paper, trying to catch up on current events.

Twenty minutes later, the taxi stopped in front of Sam's office. Sam stepped out of the taxi and said, "Give me a few minutes, and I'll be right back." The driver nodded his head in approval. Sam still had a problem. She didn't have a key. With her strength, opening the door would not be a problem, however, the mess and noise she was about to create might.

Just as she was about to bust the door open, a voice behind her asked, "Sam, is that you?"

Sam knew exactly who it was. She turned around and yelled out, "Portagee, I've missed you." She gave him a big hug. Before she could say anything else, the driver tapped on his sideview mirror.

Sam looked at Portagee and asked, "Can I borrow a twenty to pay the taxi? I left my money in my purse back in the Triangle."

Portagee laughed and walked over to the driver and said, "Here you go, mate. Thanks." The taxi driver took the money and drove off.

Roderick (Portagee) Madeiros, a Portuguese Bermudian, was Sam's partner in the detective agency. Portagee had never found his growth spurt. He might be only five foot six inches tall, but what he lacked in height, he made up for with his inventiveness. "Portagee," as his friends knew him, already held twenty-five patents and was always working on some strange contraption. Sometimes he made more trouble than he resolved, but in spite of that Sam would have him no other way.

Portagee unlocked the door and the two went into the office. Portagee said, "Sam, we've all missed you—especially your dad. We were afraid you were never going to come out of the Bermuda Triangle, or that vampire had turned you into one."

Sam didn't know what to say first, so she just let the first thought in her head pop out. "Well, Portagee, you might not be too far wrong."

Portagee said, "What do you mean?"

Sam didn't say a word; she just smiled, showing her canine teeth.

Portagee stepped back and tripped, falling to the floor. Sam smiled again and said, "Don't worry, Portagee. I think you're safe with me. So far I haven't had the urge to bite your neck."

Still a little hesitant, Portagee asked, "Are you sure?"

Sam replied, "I'm sure, and by the way, I was just kidding. At least I don't think I'm a vampire." She went on to tell Portagee how Zuka had bit her twice, one time in Bermuda and one time in the portal. She also told him how she had killed Zuka and how she had been experimenting with her newfound powers for the last eight months.

After she had finished, Portagee asked, "What now, Sam?"

Sam replied, "I discovered there are vampires and possibly other beasts all over the world right now, not just from our past, living in the Triangle. I know this might sound vengeful, but I'm going to hunt these blood beasts down wherever on this earth they are; then I'm going to destroy them. In fact just days ago, I killed one in the Triangle who had somehow found a portal in New Orleans. New Orleans is where I'm going first to track down these beasts and destroy them." She then asked, "What about the others and my dad?"

Portagee slowly replied, "Your dad is fine, but he never stops worrying about you. I've got some really bad news about Graham."

Sam stood up and asked, "What is it?"

Portagee walked over to her and said, "Let's both sit down." He then held her hand and said, "The night you went back into the Bermuda Triangle, a vampire killed Graham, but Graham also killed the vampire."

Sam started to cry, but in an instant her eyes turned blood red and then jet black. She yelled out, "Those bastards are going to pay for this."

Portagee had never seen this new side of Sam. He gave her a hug, which seemed to calm her down.

Sam then asked, "How are Michael and Keno?"

Portagee replied, "They're both on a humanitarian mission in the Congo to help feed and give medical attention to those remote tribes in need."

Sam was relieved they were both fine. She missed them both, but especially Michael, her longtime love interest. She thought to herself that Michael being gone meant one less heartache she would have by leaving him to go to New Orleans.

Portagee took Sam home and said he would be back the next day to take her to police headquarters so she could surprise her dad.

The next morning Sam was awakened by a knocking on her front door, which she assumed was Portagee. When she finally made it to the door and opened it, she had the surprise of her life. It was her father.

The commissioner stepped through the doorway and gave Sam a big bear hug. He looked at her with a smile and said, "Sorry, baby, for the surprise. You know Portagee can't keep a secret."

Sam was busy wiping tears from her eyes. She took her dad by his hand and they both went over to her sofa to sit down. Sam said, "I missed you most of all, Daddy." Then she hugged him.

Besides being Sam's father, Ian Savage was also the commissioner of the Bermuda Police Department. With his closest friends he still preferred to be called "Inspector." His high profile and outspoken comments in the past had placed his daughter Samantha in precarious situations, but in spite of that she loved her father dearly and valued his opinion.

The two talked for well over an hour, with Sam telling her dark story. Finally, the commissioner said, "When are you going to get back into your detective agency?"

Sam paused for a moment. She already knew he was not going to be in favor of her decision. In fact, he was going to be very outspoken about it. Sam slowly replied, "Dad, I'm not."

With a surprised look on his face, the commissioner said, "What did you say?"

Sam smiled and said, "Daddy, you heard me the first time. I know this will sound crazy and you're not going to like it, but I'm going to track down those vampires and eradicate them and their lair."

The commissioner turned red in the face and said, "The bloody hell you are. Those bastards will kill you in a second. Don't forget you've already been captured and tortured by them."

Trying to keep her composure, Sam replied, "I've been bitten and beaten by those blood beasts, and believe me, I'm not the same person anymore." She stood up and said, "Don't move, Daddy. Let me show you something." She reached down and picked up the sofa with the commissioner sitting on it and raised it over her head."

The commissioner yelled out, "What the bloody hell is going on? Put me down."

Sam obliged and set the sofa back on the floor. Still stunned, the commissioner asked, "Are you a vampire from being bitten?"

Sam replied, "No, at least I don't think so, but watch this." She closed her eyes for a second and then opened her eyelids quickly. Her eyes transformed from blood red to jet black. Then she smiled to show off her short, sharp canine teeth.

The commissioner's eyes were now wide open. He asked, "Any other surprises?"

Sam smiled and said, "Not too many more. I can jump over fifty feet high and fifty feet in distance. If you stab or shoot me, my body will repair itself over night. I haven't tried a stake through the heart yet. I've seen what happens to vampires when it's done. Not my cup of tea. So am I a vampire? I don't think so. I can be out in the daylight hours and I don't crave blood, at least not yet."

The commissioner knew now for sure he was not going to be able to stop her. He asked, "So where is my beast huntress going?"

Sam smiled and said, "I like that name, 'Beast Huntress'. The vampire I captured and killed in the Triangle told me he was from a clan in New Orleans. So that's where my hunt starts."

The commissioner added, "That's fine, but someone has got to go with you to cover your backside."

Sam snapped back, "Daddy, you're not going with me."

He laughed and said, "Baby girl, I'm too old for that. Your partner, Portagee, will go with you. He may be small, but he's a dynamo and a very quick thinker."

Sam replied, "Maybe you're right. I'll talk to him."

The commissioner stood up and gave Sam another hug. "I've got to go to work, but let's plan on dinner with Portagee tonight." He started to walk out the door and then turned back to say, "Oh, I almost forgot. My good friend, FBI Agent Derrick Storm, lives in New Orleans. If you contact him when you arrive, he'll give you a hand."

Sam replied, "Yes, Daddy." As she closed the door, she walked away thinking, "He'll never change, but I love him dearly."

Later that afternoon at the office, Sam turned to Portagee and said, "Portagee, I want to ask you a question."

Before she could finish, Portagee said, "Yes! Hell, yes!"

A little befuddled, Sam said, "You don't even know what I want to ask you."

"The commissioner already told me—yes, I will marry you." He paused for a few seconds and said, "Just kidding, Sam. Yes, I will go with you to the ends of the earth to track down and kill vampires."

Sam replied, "Good, I think."

A few hours later it was dark, and the three met at the St. George's Police Station. From there they walked down the dimly lit Water Street heading for the commissioner's favorite pub. From the shadows a dark figure leaped out shoving his way between Portagee and the commissioner. He stopped at Sam and grabbed her by the neck. "You're nothing but a freak of nature. You must die." His long claws shot out like switchblades. He tried to slash Sam's throat but missed and caught the commissioner with two of his claws in the stomach. The commissioner fell over in pain while Portagee tried to hang on to him.

As the blood beast turned back around, Sam backhanded him throwing his back against one of the stone buildings. He stood up laughing and said, "You bitch! Do you think that is going to stop me?" Then he leaped at Sam. With her lightning fast reflexes, Sam grabbed her hunting knife out of her boot. When he landed on Sam, she ran the massive blade through his heart. She rolled him off and jumped on top of him.

Sam yelled to the dying vampire, "What do you bloody devils want with me?"

In a low dying voice, he replied, "We want you dead. You're a freak of nature and your presence is a threat. Others will find you from our clan, and they will kill you."

Sam's eyes were jet black now. She yelled back, "Well, that's not going to happen tonight." She took the handle of her knife and shoved it deeper into the beast. He fought back for a second and then went still. Sam pulled out her knife and looked over at her dad and Portagee. "This is war. Do you believe me now?" she asked. Her eye colour went back to blue. She walked over to Portagee. "Let's get Daddy to the ER at the hospital."

Portagee said, "Good idea, but what about the vampire?"

Sam walked over to the vampire and picked him up by the legs and swung him around and around and let him go flying. His body landed in the middle of St. George's harbour. She looked back at the two and added, "He'll decompose over night, and the fish will help the process."

Once at the hospital, the commissioner was taken to the ER while Sam and Portagee waited outside.

Sam looked at Portagee and said, "I hope I didn't scare the hell out of you tonight. When I get mad or threatened I go through some transformations."

With a little look of concern, Portagee said, "Yeah, I did see a different Sammy tonight. But I can deal with it."

Sam asked, "Are you sure you're up for dealing with these beasts? They're quick, and they're deadly."

Portagee replied, "Not a problem, mate. I've run into these dirt-bags before. Since then I've invented a few contraptions to slow these bloodsuckers down. Now I'll get my chance to use them. When are we going to leave?"

Sam replied, "I'm pretty sure that blood beast followed me out of the Tri-angle, but others might have known what he was doing and where he was. If that's the case let's go to them before they come to us. Let's see if we can get a flight to Atlanta tomorrow afternoon with a connection to New Orleans."

Portagee replied, "Sounds like a plan to me. You go see how your dad's doing and get him back home, and I'll go take care of the flight arrangements and a place to stay." The two shook hands and went on their ways.

Blood Fangs

SAMANTHA SAVAGE
BEAST HUNTRESS

CHAPTER 4

The Mysterious City

THE MYSTERIOUS CITY

Two days later, Sam and Portagee were on the tarmac at the Bermuda International Airport waiting to take off to Atlanta. Sam had waited until the commissioner was at home recovering from his slash wounds.

Sam looked over at Portagee. "Hey, I've been dying to ask you something."

Portagee replied, "So go for it."

Sam continued, "So how the hell did you get your gadgets past security? I kept waiting for you to get arrested."

Laughingly, Portagee said, "Your dad shipped them out for me. No questions asked. By the time we get to New Orleans, my package will be there waiting for me."

Sam shook her head and said, "Even when he's in the hospital, he can't stay out of my business."

Portagee replied, "Well, this time you should be glad he did." Sam smiled and looked out the window as the jet lifted off the ground.

As the jet gained altitude, Sam began to get uncomfortable. She was getting slightly claustrophobic, but she did not want to let on to Portagee that there was a problem. She tried to hang on until the fasten seat belt light went out, so she could go into the restroom and try to compose herself. After waiting for another twenty minutes the fasten seat belt light finally went out. Portagee was already snoring. He never noticed Sam's anxious trip to the restroom. Sam smiled as she passed the flight attendant, but she could hardly focus on getting into the restroom. Once inside, she quickly locked the door. She flushed the toilet a couple of times trying to drown out the painful sounds she was making. So far she had been able to control herself, but she was now losing the fight. Her eyes went blood red and then jet black. She felt a pain running from her chest into her arms. Sam managed to muffle her scream. Her arms were stretched across the small restroom with both hands pressing hard against the walls.

A few minutes later she was awakened from her trance by a knock on the door. The flight attendant said, "Is everything all right in there?"

Sam blurted out, "I'm fine. I just tripped and bumped into the sink. I'll be right out."

"All right" replied the flight attendant. Sam could hear her move away.

She tried to compose herself, but she quickly found her fingernails were stuck in the walls. She pried her hands free only to find her fingernails had grown about one inch long. The way her nails pierced the walls, they must have been hard as steel. She thought to herself, "Oh great, now I've got claws like the blood beasts do, but at least they're much shorter." She began to relax and her nails receded back to normal length. Sam was relieved about that. She hated long fingernails, but she couldn't help wondering what other surprises were in store for her.

A few minutes later, she sat down next to Portagee. The movement caused Portagee to open his eyes. He looked at Sam, smiled, and fell back to sleep.

Upon arriving in New Orleans, Portagee hailed a taxi to take them downtown.

Later that night, Portagee and Sam met out in front of their hotel.

Sam looked at Portagee and said, "Are you packing?"

Portagee smiled and said, "You bet! My gadgets were waiting for me in the hotel room. I brought holy water guns, a laser ink pen, flash grenades, and a wrist blaster. I'm ready to rock and roll."

Sam replied, "Don't even tell me what all this stuff is for. I think I'm better off not knowing."

"Okay, I know we're going to the French Quarter, but where do we start?" Portagee asked.

Sam replied, "Once we hit a few bars, those blood beasts will find us, my friend. But just in case we're going to visit a few Voodoo shops in the Bourbon Street area first. Now let's get going. We've got a twenty-minute walk to get there."

It was still early in the evening by the time Portagee and Sam made their way down into the French Quarter. As they walked past bar after bar Portagee asked repeatedly, "What about this bar?"

Sam finally snapped back at Portagee. "Look, buddy, it's the Voodoo shops first and the bars second. What part of that can you not understand, Portagee?"

Portagee replied, "Sorry, Sam. I'm just anxious to step into one of these pubs and drink a hurricane."

Sam laughed and said, "You drink one of those, Portagee, and I'll find you in the swamps playing with the gators."

Portagee smiled and said, "Well, crap!"

The two kept walking down Bourbon Street. Finally, after walking several blocks, Sam looked down a side street and then nudged Portagee in the arm. "Look, mate. Down this street I see what looks like a Voodoo shop." The two walked closer to the store and sure enough it was a Voodoo store. The name on the store was Zombie Death Walker. The two walked into the store. It was so small and crowded that Portagee had to walk behind Sam. Portagee was sidetracked by the shrunken heads, hundreds of bottles of potions, lit candles, and hundreds of objects that he could not identify.

While Portagee was wandering around the shop, Sam went up to the counter at the back of the store and tapped on the glass counter.

A few minutes later, a small black man came out from behind a doorway covered with beads on strings. He had white streaks of paint on his face, and he was wearing what looked like a multicolored bedsheet around him. He walked up to Sam and said, "Young lady, what is it I can help you with?"

Sam looked back at him and said, "I'm looking for vampire clans to make contact with."

The small man looked at her and laughed. "There are no clans here in the city, or for that matter, anywhere else. If you want gators, go out into the swamps tomorrow. They'll be more than happy to visit with you." He then set a bottle of lotion on the table and said, "Pour some of this on their tails, and they'll let you rub their tummies."

Sam was pissed at his answer. She reached across the counter and lifted him up over her head. Her eyes turned blood red to jet black in seconds. Next, her fingernails grew an inch sticking into the man's neck, but not breaking the skin. She then smiled showing her small canines. Sam drew him closer to her face and said, "Little man, what did you just say to me? Do you think for a moment that I already don't know about beast clans in New Orleans?"

The shopkeeper was now fearful for his life. He thought Sam was a vampire from a clan from somewhere else. Sam shook him a couple more times and said, "Portagee, lock the front door. I'm getting thirsty."

Portagee was shocked at Sam's behavior, but he did what he was told anyway.

The shopkeeper was now frantic as Sam pulled his neck to her mouth. He screamed out, "I don't know any beasts, but the Voodoo Queen might!"

Sam dropped him to the floor and with her foot on his chest yelled, "Where the hell does this Voodoo Queen live?"

The shopkeeper blurted out, "She's just four blocks from here. Just down Bourbon Street. She thinks she's a direct descendent of the first Voodoo Queen of New Orleans."

Sam snapped back, "Well, she may just be the last descendent of the Voodoo Queen when I get finished with her." She looked over at Portagee and added, "Tie this bloody bastard up or I might decide to stay and drain his life's blood from him."

Portagee did so without question, but he was becoming troubled by Sam's aggressiveness.

As they left the shop, Sam turned to Portagee. "Let's go find this Voodoo Queen now," she said.

Portagee grabbed her by the arm and said, "Now wait just a bloody minute. We're not going anywhere except to the first bar we find. You and I are going to have a long talk." Sam was surprised at Portagee's outburst, but she agreed to take a break at one of the local bars.

SAMANTHA SAVAGE
BEAST HUNTRESS

CHAPTER 5

The Voodoo Queen

THE VOODOO QUEEN

Not long after leaving the Voodoo shop they found a small pub that was almost deserted. This would be the perfect spot to allow them some privacy.

As they sipped on their beers, Portagee asked, "Sam, what in the hell is the matter with you? You're almost out of control. I'm beginning to think you're part vampire or at least have the tendencies of one."

Sam smiled and replied, "There is no bloody way in hell I'm a vampire." Although she had those same thoughts, she would never admit them. She continued, "Portagee, I know I'm not the same person I was a year ago, but there's nothing I can do about it. I've spent the last eight months trying to find out who I am and discover my new powers, but sometimes it's hard to control myself. I was just trying to scare the hell out of the Voodoo shopkeeper. I wasn't going to drink his blood." Or was she?

A short time later, Sam and Portagee made their way down Bourbon Street to the Voodoo Queen's shop. It didn't take long for Sam to realize that they were being followed. Sam leaned over to Portagee and whispered, "I sense we're being followed."

Portagee looked around and then back at Sam and said, "Girl, I think you're just nervous. There's not a soul following us."

Sam replied, "You're right about that. There's no one with a soul following us."

Portagee turned back to Sam. "What the hell does that mean?"

Sam snapped back, "I sense something undead like a vampire or some other type of night beast." Her instincts kicked in. Her eyes went black and her nails grew an inch long.

Looking at Sam, Portagee exclaimed, "Holy crap!"

Before Portagee could say anything else, a dark figure stepped out in front of them. Portagee stuck out one arm in front of Sam and said, "Stop! I'll take care of this." He lifted his other arm and pointed his hand directly at the dark figure. Next he flipped his wrist in an upward motion and a wood dart fired out from under his shirt cuff in a split second.

The dark figure let out a scream and then stepped out of the darkness. The dart was sticking through his ear lobe. Sam looked at Portagee and said, "Good shot, mate. Fire another dart into his other ear and give him a matching set of earrings."

A bit embarrassed, Portagee yelled out, "Sam, run!" He then reached into his coat pocket and pulled out a flash grenade. He pulled the pin and threw it at the feet of the beast. Upon impact, the grenade exploded, creating a silent blast of light energy. The blood beast disintegrated in burning ash in seconds.

Sam turned around at that same moment, grabbed Portagee, and leaped to the upper balcony of the building. The second they landed, both of them laid down on the decking and waited to see what would happen next.

A few seconds later, a second blood beast arrived and screamed out to another dark figure, "Where in the hell did those humans go?"

The other figure just stood there and said nothing in return. The blood beast went on to say, "You dumb bastard! Take my pet and track them down." The vampire was speaking to the zombie and his pet, a swamp beast, a type of chupacabras. Just like vampires, no one believes swamp chupacabras exist. These beasts are as big as a medium-sized dog but more vicious than a much larger wolf. They have extended front teeth, which are followed by razor sharp shark-like teeth. This vampire clan had turned swamp chupacabras into the perfect swamp trackers. There's nothing in the massive swamps of Louisiana that these beasts can't track and find. These beasts spend as much time in the water as out of the water. They can track the smell of blood in or out of the water. In a state of hunger, even vampires have a difficult time controlling these swamp chupacabras. With their massive front teeth and supporting shark teeth, they can rip their victims to pieces in seconds. Even swamp gators steer clear of these bloodsucking scaly beasts, which have sharp spikes running down their backbones. These beasts were brought in from Puerto Rico over a hundred years ago by vampires and have no resemblance to their distant cousins, the Texas and Mexican chupacabras.

The zombie and the swamp chupacabras went down the next alley trying to pick up the scent of their prey while the vampire stayed in place under the balcony where Sam and Portagee were hiding. The vampire could sense their presence, but he could not detect them. A minute later, he ran down the same alley that the zombie had run down.

Once Sam knew they were in the clear she sat up. She said, "What in the hell was that beast the vampire had?"

Portagee replied, "I don't know, but this is one dark alley I don't want to meet him in. That other man with the vampire appeared to be stoned."

Sam added, "Portagee, don't forget where we are. We're looking for a Voodoo Queen right now. I'm guessing that dude was stoned, but not by his own free will. I bet Voodoo had something to do with this."

Portagee replied, "Well, that makes it worse then. The Voodoo believers must be working with the vampires."

Sam stood up and said, "Let's go. We've need to find this Voodoo Queen."

As Portagee stood up, he asked, "Good, but are we going to jump off the balcony to get down?"

Sam replied, "Hell no!" She walked over to the balcony door, opened it up, and then she walked through it. "See you downstairs, mate. You can jump if you want," she said.

Portagee fired back, "No, I'm with you." He quickly followed her through the doorway, down a set of stairs, and back out into the street.

Once on the street, Sam turned to Portagee and said, "Let's not go the same way our friends went. We'll walk a couple of extra blocks and circle back to the shop. Otherwise they may be waiting for us. I want to find this Voodoo Queen and see if she is the real deal."

Meanwhile not far from Sam and Portagee, Queen Delphine, the Voodoo Queen, was in her shop. Being a Voodoo Queen was just a front for Delphine. She was really the queen of the vampire clan that made New Orleans their home. She was the oldest member of the clan of blood beasts. It was thought that she was over two hundred years old. None of the other vampires really knew because she herself had turned every member in the clan into a vampire at one time or another. Although she never admitted it to any other beast in the clan, they believed her to be Marie Delphine LaLaurie, a once infamous socialite in New Orleans from the eighteen hundreds. Delphine was a white Creole with long flowing shiny black hair. Her mesmerizing beauty could stop a herd of stampeding horses. There wasn't a man in New Orleans who would not fall for her in a heartbeat. She would entertain and have elaborate parties, frequently at her mansion in the French Quarter. It was also reported that she was well acquainted with the first Voodoo Queen of New Orleans, Marie Laveau.

In her time, Marie Delphine LaLaurie was one of the most viciously evil women to have ever lived in America. She was a slave owner and was known to torture her slaves in the dungeon of her mansion. If she were to become a vampire this is where she would have cultivated her blood lust. There were reports that she would pluck eyes from her slaves and even decapitate them before hacking them up into tiny pieces. Delphine's sadistic practices went unchecked for years in her hidden torture chamber until one day in 1834 a fire broke out in her mansion. It was believed that one of her slaves had started the fire to expose her atrocities to the people of New Orleans. The fire caused severe damage to the mansion, exposing the torture chamber and the mutilated slaves she had kept in hiding. A vigilante mob hellbent on killing Delphine descended on her mansion. Just before the mob's arrival, she escaped in a horse-drawn carriage. It is believed that she fled to France where she died of old age. Some believe she fled through a secret dimensional portal, which allowed her to escape into another parallel world and return when she wanted. Whether she fled or not, after the death of her acquaintance the Voodoo Queen Marie Laveau in 1881, a new Voodoo Queen by the name of Delphine appeared. To this date, Voodoo believers think the Voodoo Queen Delphine comes from a long line of descendants of the original Voodoo Queen Delphine. However, the vampire clan knows that Delphine is the original queen, who every twenty or thirty years transforms her appearance to become a new Queen Delphine. Being a Voodoo Queen has been the perfect cover for Delphine. She can move among the people in the dark hours of night in the French Quarter without creating any suspicions. Delphine is an extremely powerful blood beast. Coupled with her Voodoo knowledge, she remains unchallenged in her clan.

The vampire who had been tracking Sam and Portagee entered the Voodoo shop. Delphine turned to the vampire and said, "What have you to report to me, my love?"

Nervously, the vampire replied, "My queen, I lost them. They discovered we were following them and they eluded us."

Delphine impatiently fired back, "You lost them even while using a swamp chupacabras to track them?"

The vampire replied, "Yes."

In a split second Delphine was over the store display counter and in the face of the vampire. With one of her two-inch nails on her right hand, she clawed the nail down the side of his face. As the blood flowed down his face, she leaned in and licked the fresh gash. Then she said, "I'm of the mind to drain your blood now and be done with you. Is that what you want, my slave?"

Now trembling the vampire replied, "No, my queen."

Delphine took some powder from a pouch on her belt and blew it into the face of the vampire. A few seconds later she said, "Go find these strange visitors and bring them to me. Should you fail, take this knife and slit your throat." She placed a razor-sharp dagger in his hand. Then she asked, "Do you understand?"

In a slight trance, the vampire said, "Yes, my queen." He then turned and left the Voodoo shop.

Blood Fangs

SAMANTHA SAVAGE
BEAST HUNTRESS

CHAPTER 6

City of the Dead

CITY OF THE DEAD

Twenty minutes later, Sam and Portagee opened the door to the Voodoo shop, not knowing they were stepping into a vampires' den of death.

Sam walked up to the counter where a clerk was standing and said, "Hi, I'm here to see the Voodoo Queen."

The clerk looked her and Portagee over and replied, "Just a minute. I'll see if she's in." She turned and walked through the door parting the beaded curtain. Once in the back room, she walked up to Delphine and said, "My queen, you have visitors."

Delphine looked at the security monitor, and she could not believe her eyes. It was the pair her clan was looking for. What good fortune! She felt the blood rushing through her body, causing her eyes to turn blood red. She knew if she went out to talk to the pair her cover might be blown. She reached down and picked up a pair of sunglasses that had very dark lenses. As soon as she put them on she replied, "Very well. I'll see them."

Delphine left the back room and went into the retail shop. Walking up to Sam, she said, "Good evening, what can Queen Delphine do for you tonight?"

Sam smiled and said, "Yes, my name is Samantha Savage, and I've just arrived in New Orleans. I was told that you're an expert on zombies and vampires."

Delphine replied, "I am the Voodoo Queen of New Orleans, but nothing more."

Sam replied, "Yes, I know that, but I'm following up on a lead about blood beast folklore in New Orleans."

Delphine's senses were starting to overpower her. Her fingernails were beginning to grow. She tried to conceal them by folding her arms. Finally, she said, "My dear, maybe you should go visit our local city of the dead."

Sam asked, "Where is this city of the dead?"

Portagee interrupted. "Sam, I think it's time to go."

Sam snapped back, "Well, I'm not ready to leave." She turned back around and to her surprise Delphine was gone. At that same moment, several customers entered the shop.

Portagee grabbed her by the arm and said, "Come on, Sam. Let's get out of here." Once outside, Portagee looked at her and said, "Sam, cities of the dead are cemeteries."

Sam rolled her eyes. "That bitch played me for a fool. Why did she do that? Do you think she knew what we were up to?"

As they walked away from the shop, Portagee said, "Look, mate, she told us to go to a cemetery. There's one close by. You game?"

Sam replied, "Are you crazy? That city of the dead will be full of zombies and bloodsuckers."

Portagee said, "I thought that's what we're here for—to find vampires."

Sam stepped up her walking pace and said, "Let's do it, but little man, you'd better be ready to face some badasses."

Portagee replied, "Not to worry. Let's go."

Meanwhile, back at the Voodoo shop, Delphine had summoned two of her vampire lieutenants, Jock and Duba. They met her in the back room of the Voodoo shop. Delphine handed them a picture and said, "My security camera took this picture of these two. The young girl's name is Samantha

Savage. I have no idea who her male companion is. This is the woman we discovered in the Bermuda Triangle, but she escaped. We were trying to find her in Bermuda, and out of nowhere, she has shown up in New Orleans. Not only that, but she appears to be looking for us."

Jock asked, "Does she know anything?"

Delphine replied, "She knows something. She's here, isn't she?"

Duba added, "We'll just track them down and kill them. I'm thirsty for blood."

Delphine snapped back, "You idiot! I want to know why they are here and what they know. Besides, she may not be so easy to kill. She's not human and not vampire. I sensed she's some type of hybrid. Frankly, I don't know what she is. Maybe she's a day walker, but there's never been one documented. The male is a human. If he doesn't know anything, feed him to the swamp chupacabras. I want the girl alive or at least not dead. Do you understand?"

Both vampires nodded their heads in agreement and left the shop.

Sam and Portagee had almost reached the gates of St. Louis Cemetery No. 1, a cemetery within walking distance of the French Quarter. Cemeteries in New Orleans are called "cities of the dead" due to the ground water saturation level, which causes the dead to have to be buried above ground. The mausoleums and crypts from the air appear to be miniature ivory and concrete cities. The St. Louis Cemetery No. 1 is one of the oldest cities of the dead in New Orleans.

As they walked up to the gate of the cemetery, Portagee asked, "What now, where do we start?"

Sam stepped closer to the gate and said, "Wait just a second. Let me scan the area." Sam used her bat sonar senses to scan a large area of the cemetery for movement of any type. Once done, she said, "All is clear, Portagee, except for some squirrels and birds."

A surprised Portagee said, "What the bloody hell did you just do, mate?"

Sam snapped back, "We don't need night vision goggles because I ust scanned about one hundred yards into the cemetery with my sonar brain waves."

Portagee said, "So let's go in, but where?"

Sam replied, "I know the first Voodoo Queen of New Orleans, Marie Laveau, is buried in this cemetery. Let's visit her tomb first."

Portagee walked over to the gate and pushed it open. "Ladies first."

Sam smiled and said, "Such a gentleman. I feel so safe."

Portagee replied, "All right, but you're the one with sonar." Portagee walked through the gate first and pulled what appeared to be a weapon out of his jacket pocket.

As Sam followed him, she asked, "Since when did you start packing?"

Portagee looked at her and said, "It's not a real pistol, but it will be just as effective. It's a water gun filled with holy water."

Sam shook her head in doubt and replied, "Oh brother! Those blood beasts are going to think you're trying to give them a bath."

Portagee smiled and said, "We'll see." They continued to walk in the direction of Marie Laveau's tomb.

Meanwhile, Jock and Duba and several other vampires arrived at the cemetery with their swamp chupacabras.

Duba looked at the other vampires and said, "Let's give these humans a real welcome to New Orleans. Release the swamp chupacabras." The vampires did as they were told and unleashed their two swamp chupacabras. In seconds, they disappeared into the darkness of the night.

Duba added, "Now all we have to do is follow the screams. Let's go, but spread out just in case they're not together or in case the swamp chupacabras split them up." The vampires walked down different paths in search of their prey.

Not far away, Sam and Portagee came upon Marie Laveau's tomb. After looking at it for a few minutes in the light of the moon, Portagee asked, "What are these triple x's marked all over the tomb?"

Sam replied, "If I remember right, they are from visitors hoping the spirit of Marie Laveau will grant them a wish." Sam also noticed a series of numbers written on the side of the tomb in an obscure place. They were just under the roof line of the tomb.

Before Sam could say anything, Portagee asked, "May I borrow a pen? I think we could use a wish right now."

Sam snapped back, "That's defacing a tomb. Do you want to get us in trouble?"

In a low tone, Portagee laughed and said, "Oh yeah, like we're not already in big trouble now." Before either of them could say anything else, they heard something moving in their direction very quickly.

Sam never got a chance to use her senses. Out of nowhere, one of the swamp chupacabras leaped on Portagee's back, biting and clawing at his neck. Portagee swung around in circles trying to knock the beast off his back, but to no avail. Finally, Sam grabbed the beast by his thick tail and flung him against Marie Laveau's tomb, crushing the swamp chupacabra and leaving blood all over the side of the tomb.

Portagee looked at the blood and said, "I think we can forget the spirit granting us any wishes now. You just made her tomb look like hell."

Sam looked at Portagee and said, "Shut up! Are you hurt?" Sam then sensed more bodies closing in on them from all directions. She grabbed Portagee by the arm and jumped on top of the tomb.

Once on the tomb, Portagee jerked his arm back and said, "Would you quit doing that?"

Sam ignored his comment and said, "In a few seconds we'll be surrounded. We can't hide, but maybe we'll be able to defend ourselves better from here."

A few seconds later, they were surrounded by figures shining flashlights in their faces. Sam leaned over to Portagee and said, "Go ahead. Try you squirt gun now."

Portagee stepped aside and raised his gun to point it at the figure standing in front of the tomb. The figure yelled out, "You pull that trigger, and you're a dead man. I've got enough fire power here with the New Orleans police department to blow you to hell and back. Now drop the pistol!" Portagee complied and dropped the gun to the ground. The figure said, "Identify yourself!"

Sam spoke up first. "Samantha Savage."

Before Portagee could say anything, the figure stepped forward and said, "Sam, is that you and Portagee?"

Sam was surprised. She replied, "Yes, but who the hell are you?"

The figure replied, "It's me, Special Agent Derek Storm."

Special Agent Derek Storm was dark skinned, forty-five years old, and six feet one inch tall with a medium large build. He also held a black belt in karate.

Sam could not believe what she had just heard. Derek Storm was not only an FBI agent, but he was her dad's best friend. On several occasions he had been to Bermuda to work on cases with her dad.

Sam replied, "Oh, thank God!"

Storm asked, "Would you two come down?"

Sam and Portagee both jumped down from the tomb. As Storm walked over to them, one of the officers walked over to him and handed him Portagee's pistol. Storm looked at it in disbelief. "Portagee, what the hell were you thinking? A water pistol? You almost got shot over a water pistol."

A little embarrassed, Portagee responded, "Sorry sir. It's a long story."

Storm replied, "Don't worry. You'll have time to tell me all about it back at the station." He then looked at the side of the tomb and asked, "Whose blood is all over this tomb? Don't tell me you made someone bleed with that water pistol."

Sam spoke up. "A bloody beast attacked us, and I smashed him against the tomb wall."

Storm looked around and asked, "Where is this beast? All I see is a blood-smeared tomb."

Sam didn't want to say anything more in front of the other officers. She held out her arms and said, "Cuff us, Storm."

Storm didn't know whether to laugh or get pissed. He said, "You two come with me. We're going to a small padded room back at the police station." Sam and Portagee left the cemetery with Storm. The vampires had seen Storm and the New Orleans police arrive on the scene and had quickly disappeared in the dark of the night.

Blood Fangs

SAMANTHA SAVAGE
BEAST HUNTRESS

CHAPTER 7

Dark n Stormy

DARK N STORMY

Back at the New Orleans police department, Storm made good on his word. They were in a padded room with no one-way glass walls. Sam and Portagee were sitting on one side of the table while Storm was on the other side. Storm looked at Sam and Portagee and said, "You two are damn lucky your dad called and let me know you were going on a witch hunt."

Sam fired back, "What the hell do you mean, witch hunt?"

Storm said, "Look, missy, you sit there and be quiet and let me do the talking." Sam bit her tongue and nodded her head in agreement. Storm went on to say, "We're in this room for a reason. I don't want anyone listening to us, and even though you two could be charged with defacing a landmark tomb, there will be no charges. Your dad told me why you're here. If I didn't already know some of the strange adventures you two have been through, I would throw the two of you to the wolves. But vampires, are you kidding?"

There was a long pause and then Sam stood up and said, "Let me show you something." She leaned over the desk staring into Storm's eyes as her eyes went from blue to blood red and then jet black. At the same time, her fingernails grew almost an inch long. As she sat back down in her chair, she said, "Oh, I almost forgot." Then she smiled, showing off her sharp canines.

Portagee added, "Don't look at me, mate. I can't do any of that. I just have a squirt gun loaded with holy water. By the way, when do I get my gun back?"

Storm was in shock; he didn't know what to say. He finally said, "Sam, are you a vampire?"

Sam smiled. Her teeth back to normal and no canines were showing. She replied, "No, at least I don't think so, but I have been bitten."

Storm went on to ask, "So what were you doing in the cemetery?"

Portagee replied, "The Voodoo Queen said we would find answers there."

Storm added, "You better be careful with the Queen. She is revered as the true queen of New Orleans and her believers will do her bidding. So what answers were you looking for? Maybe I can help."

Sam looked at Portagee and then back at Storm. "Agent Storm, you're an honorable man, but I'm here on a mission that you cannot be a part of. We appreciate your help and concern, but it has to stop here. I will be more careful going forward and try not to draw attention to us, but my destiny is cast." She looked back at Portagee and said, "You can still turn back if you want, but I have to go on now."

As she got up and left the room, Portagee yelled out, "You're not dumping me that easy! Wait up." He gave Storm a thumbs up and went running after Sam.

Storm just sat there. He could tell his best friend's daughter was about to stir up one hell of a hornet's nest. Somehow he would have to find out what she was up to. Finally, Storm jumped up and yelled out the doorway, "It will be daylight soon. I hope you won't get a sunburn." He already knew no one heard him, but at least he had said something. Then he left the police station because he needed a walk to think his options over.

Back at the Voodoo shop, Delphine was surprised to see her henchmen back so soon. She looked at them and asked, "So where in hell are these humans?"

Jock slowly replied, "They got away from us, my queen."

Delphine screamed back, "What in hell do you mean, they got away? You had them out numbered five to one with two swamp chupacabras, and they still got away?"

Jock tried to reply. "The girl killed one of the swamp chupacabras with her hands. The next thing we knew the New Orleans police were all over the cemetery."

In disgust Delphine walked over to Jock. She put a hand on each side of his face. Then she tipped his neck back and dug her fangs deep into his throat. Blood sprayed in all directions. Jock yelled in agony. A few seconds later, Delphine stepped back, removing her fangs from his neck. She looked him in the eyes and said, "I cannot tolerate idiots." Without allowing Jock to reply, she snapped his head off with sheer force. His body collapsed to the floor and Delphine tossed his head down next to his body. Delphine looked at the others and said, "Are you going to follow my instructions next time?" She didn't wait for answers. She abruptly turned and walked toward the shop's back door. As she left, she said, "Keep an eye on the shop. I'm going home before sunrise." She closed the door behind her and in an instant she was gone from sight.

Meanwhile back in her hotel room, Sam was busy scanning through screen after screen on her laptop. It was now early morning, and she was surprised to hear a knock at her door this early. She yelled out. "It's open, Portagee. Come on in."

Portagee opened the door and entered the room with a surprised look on his face. He asked Sam, "Why the hell did you leave your door unlocked, and how did you know it was me?"

Sam smiled and replied, "First of all, anyone who enters this room is taking his own life in his hands, and I sensed it was you anyway."

Portagee replied back, "Well, at least you're comfortable with all this sinister dark shadow stuff." He looked over at Sam, who was keying on her laptop and asked, "So why in hell are you on the laptop this early? Checking your social networks?"

Sam snapped back, "Get a life, Portagee. I don't social network with anyone. Anyway, back at Marie Laveau's tomb I remember seeing a series of numbers engraved on the tomb. I think it was a GPS location, and I'm trying to locate where it's at."

Portagee shook his head and then said, "So now you're going to tell me you have a photographic memory?"

Sam smiled as she typed. "Pretty much." As she kept on typing Portagee closed and locked the door and sat down next to her on the sofa watching. A few minutes later she turned the screen toward Portagee and said, "Damn, I'm good. Look. It was a GPS location. It's a two-hundred-year-old plantation out in the middle of nowhere in a swamp."

Portagee asked, "Who the bloody hell would want to live on an old run-down plantation in a swamp?"

Sam smiled and said, "Oh, I can't think of anyone except for maybe a bloodsucking vampire! What better place to hide?"

Portagee added, "Sam, that's what I like about you. You're so bloody smart. Now don't tell me we're going to spend the day in a humid gator-filled swamp today?"

Sam replied, "Well, I don't know about you, but I would rather be there in the daylight than the twilight."

Portagee scratched his head and said, "Daylight's burning, baby. Let's go get a rental car and go for a ride in the country—I mean the swamp."

Sam shut the lid on her laptop, stood up, and walked toward the door. As she walked out the door, she said, "Are you coming, Portagee?" She added, "Oh, if you ever call me baby again, I'll kick your ass."

As she walked down the hallway, Portagee ran after her and yelled out, "Point taken."

Blood Fangs

SAMANTHA SAVAGE
BEAST HUNTRESS

CHAPTER 8

Black Bayou Plantation

BLACK BAYOU PLANTATION

After finding their way out of New Orleans, they drove north out of the city for almost an hour. Finally, they came across an old parish road that Sam was sure would lead them to the plantation.

Portagee was driving. He looked down the old gravel road that appeared to disappear into the swamp and asked, "Sam, are you sure you want to go down this road? It's a single-lane road, and it might be a one-way trip for us."

Sam looked at Portagee and said, "I can feel it. The blood beasts are somewhere down this old road and there's no turning back. We've come too far to stop now."

Portagee replied, "Well, bloody hell then, let's go before it gets dark."

Sam looked at him and said, "Please do."

Portagee stepped on the accelerator and the car took off down the road throwing gravel out behind its tires. It was now midafternoon and there would be no way Sam and Portagee would be out of the Black Bayou swamp before dark.

The drive became very slow for them. The swamp was now on both sides of the narrow gravel road. However, for Sam and Portagee the drive was very mysterious. There was a beauty in the swamp. The green cypress trees rising out of the waters of the swamp and the Spanish moss clinging to the tree branches were breathtaking. The wildlife was alive and moving all around them. The herons and egrets were along the shoreline and high in the trees. Occasionally they could see gators slipping down into the water as their car approached them.

As they drove farther into the swamp, the trees became denser and the sunlight above the swamp roof was beginning to get blocked out. The beauty of the swamp was slowly dying away as they drove deeper into it.

It was now late afternoon, but Sam was determined to find the plantation even though she was concerned about the time of day. Portagee could see the anxiety in her face. He asked her, "Sam, why don't we turn back and start earlier in the morning to find this plantation?"

Sam shook her head and said, "I can't turn back, but I'll understand if you want to."

Portagee snapped back, "There's no way in hell I'm leaving you behind. We'll keep going."

A short time later, the car turned a sharp curve. The road was lined on both sides with cypress trees and swamp. Several hundred yards down the road a massive plantation stood out like a dark castle. As they approached the plantation it appeared increasingly eerie. The paint on the siding of the plantation had been worn off years ago. The few shutters that were still hanging by the windows were either severely damaged or hanging at angles.

Portagee stopped the car just before the entrance gate leading into the plantation. He looked over at Sam and said, "Holy crap! This looks like my worst nightmare. Can I call the Bermuda Regiment to come help us?"

Sam replied, "I've got a better idea, my friend."

Portagee asked, "Oh yeah, what's that?"

Sam pointed out the car window and said, "Pull the car over there out of sight, and turn it around. I want us to be pointing in the direction of the way out of here just in case we're in a hurry."

Portagee replied, "That's a damn good idea." In a minute he had the car turned around. Both of them got out of the car and walked through the entrance and onto the grounds of the plantation. Portagee looked at Sam and said, "Now what?"

Sam frowned at Portagee and said, "What are you here for? Do I have to do everything for you? Let's take the direct approach. I'll go knock on the front door, and you walk around the back to see what you can find."

Portagee agreed and walked around the back of the plantation while Sam walked up the old broken-down stairs that led up to the porch and the front door.

As Sam made her way to the front door of the mansion, Portagee went snooping around the back. Sam knocked on the door and waited for a minute and then knocked again. A minute later, the door opened. A pale-looking man with his hair pulled in a ponytail was standing in the doorway. He just stood there and stared at Sam. Finally, Sam asked, "Is this the home of Delphine the Voodoo Queen?"

The man just continued standing there without saying a word.

Trying to be polite, Sam said, "Did you hear me?"

Another man stepped into the doorway and replied, "He can't speak. What do you want?"

Sam thought to herself, "Why in hell is he answering the door?" Then she asked, "Is Delphine here?"

The man replied, "Yes, come in please." He stepped back to the side and motioned Sam to come in.

Sam stepped through the doorway and into the entryway, but before she could say anything she saw a fist flying through the air directly at her face. It was too late to avoid the fist. The blow to the side of her face sent her flying backwards. She crashed through the screen door, landing on her butt. A much bigger man stepped through the doorway and said, "Day walker, get up off your ass. I'm going to break you in half."

Sam had never been called a day walker before, but it didn't matter. She slowly stood up, shaking the cobwebs out of her head.

The big man laughed and said, "Bitch, come to poppa."

Sam was now pissed. She shook her head. Her fiery eyes went blood red to jet black in an instant. She couldn't keep her fangs from showing as she leaped at the man. With her right fist she threw an uppercut that struck the man in the chin and sent him sailing back into his two mates. Before any of them could hit the floor, Sam was on them like flies on stink. They never knew what hit them. Sam elbowed the pale man in the face, sending him crashing through a nearby stair rail. She side-kicked the other man so hard he crashed halfway through the front window, which left him hung up on the glass still in the window. She then took her claws and slashed at the chest of the big man, causing him to scream in agony. Next she looked him straight in the eyes and shouted, "So much for southern hospitality, you big Cajun bastard!"

The big man tried to throw another punch at Sam, but this time she was ready. She grabbed his fist with both of her hands and did a flip with her entire body. All you could hear were the bones in the big goon's arm snapping in half. When she landed back on her feet, she kneed him in his face and sent him backwards. He landed flat on his back halfway through the doorway. Sam walked to the doorway only to see Portagee standing there.

Portagee looked at the body lying at his feet and looked back up at Sam. He said, "What is it with you? Do you always have to have a grand entry before I get here?"

Sam wasn't laughing. She was in pain. The big goon's punch had hurt her. She looked at Portagee and said, "This big bastard called me a day walker. How the hell did he know about us?"

Portagee stepped over the big man as he entered the house. He looked at Sam and said, "It's going to take a lot of makeup to cover that shiner on your face. Tomorrow you're going to have one hell of a black eye. Are you all right?"

Sam snapped back, "Yes, I'm fine." She went on to say, "No man is going to mark me. When I wake up, I'll be fine."

Portagee looked around and said, "It almost looks like they were waiting for us. Do you think it was a trap?"

Sam replied, "They knew about us all right, but if it was a trap there would have been more of them. Not just these three goons. Since we're inside, let's look around. The goon did say Delphine was here."

Portagee added, "Yeah, it is tea time. Maybe she's having tea on the veranda."

Sam replied, "I don't think so. I just made enough noise to wake the dead. So I'm guessing no one is upstairs."

Portagee looked at Sam and said, "Oh crap, you want to look downstairs, don't you?"

Sam nodded her head and said, "Yeah, let's see if we can wake the undead."

The two looked around for thirty minutes, but could not find any door that led downstairs. Finally, Portagee said, "You know we're in a swamp. Maybe there is no cellar in this house. Otherwise it would be full of water."

Sam was doubtful. "I hear what you're saying, but this house is sitting on a stone foundation and not up on stilts or blocks. Right now it probably doesn't matter. It's almost dark, and I think we might want to get out of here just to be safe."

Portagee smiled in agreement. "Now that's a good idea."

The two quickly walked out of the house and left the property. When they got to the car, Portagee said, "Oh crap. Look at the tires." All four of the tires had been slashed and were as flat as pancakes.

Sam looked at Portagee and said, "We can change the tires. We've still got time before it gets dark."

Portagee replied, "Good idea, except for one problem."

Sam asked, "What's that?"

Portagee opened the trunk and pointed down. "Cars only come with one spare tire."

Sam slammed the trunk lid down and said, "It's a long walk out of here, but we better get our asses moving and distance ourselves from this place before it gets dark."

Portagee replied, "You don't have to tell me twice. Let's move out." The two began walking down the gravel road at a very fast pace.

Blood Farms

SAMANTHA SAVAGE
BEAST HUNTRESS

CHAPTER 9

The Swamp of Death

THE SWAMP OF DEATH

The two had walked two hundred yards down the eerie road. Finally, Portagee turned to Sam and asked, "What's wrong with this picture, Sam?"

Sam replied, "Yeah, I'm thinking the same thing. Someone slashed our tires not wanting us to leave or thinking that if we did they would be able to find us walking down this bloody road."

Portagee added, "Well, we have two options. We could go back, burn down the house, and maybe kill a few vampires, or keep walking and sooner or later they'll catch up to us."

Sam smiled and said, "Well, maybe there's another option."

Portagee asked, "What would that be?"

Sam replied, "Well, we are here to track down these blood beasts and destroy them. We couldn't find their lair in the plantation and if we wait for them, there's no assurances we'll get them before they get us. Plus whoever slashed our tires is probably still watching us—"

Portagee interrupted. "So what the hell are we going to do?"

Sam snapped back, "Be patient, mate. I'm getting to it." She went on to say, "If we're going to be the hunted, let those bloody bastards find us in the swamps."

Portagee grimaced at Sam and said, "How far are we going to get into the swamp without a boat? Not to mention the gators, snakes, and swamp chupacabras."

Sam walked over to the edge of the swamp and made two footprints in the soft ground. She looked at Portagee and said, "Don't make any more tracks. Jump onto my back, and we're going to leap out into the swamp and go from tree to tree for a few hundred yards. They'll be confused if they see only one set of tracks walking into the swamp. If we stay in the trees for a while, those bloody swamp chupacabras will have a hard time tracking us. I'm sure you can help me set a few traps for these vampires."

Portagee replied, "Sounds like a plan, but are you sure you can still leap with me on your back? It'll be like lugging a one hundred-fifty-pound bag of potatoes."

Sam smiled, "Well, maybe then I'll start calling you Spud." She turned her back to Portagee and said, "Hop on, mate, let's go."

Portagee felt uneasy about jumping on Sam's back, but he finally jumped and landed on her back. She wrapped both arms around his legs and said, "My, Portagee, I think you've gained weight."

Portagee lightly wacked her on the back of her head and said, "Enough of the small talk. Get jumping!"

Sam laughed as she flexed her knees. A second later, she leaped into the air. "Holy crap!" Portagee yelled as he hung on for dear life.

As they approached the first cypress tree, Sam said, "Be ready for one hell of a jolt when we land."

Portagee yelled back, "Now you tell me." A second later they landed on the upper branches of the tree. The sudden impact almost tossed Portagee over the top of Sam. Sam gave Portagee a moment to resettle himself and without warning leaped to another tree. This time they had a surprise waiting for them. A large white egret over three feet tall was standing on the limb that Sam was about to land on.

Sam yelled out as she waved one arm as a warning for the large bird, "Move your big bird ass!" Seconds from landing, the large, startled egret let out a loud screech and flapped its wings just clearing Sam's head by inches. With an abrupt landing, Sam looked back over her shoulder and asked, "Are you all right, Portagee?"

A little shaken, Portagee replied, "Yeah, but what's this sticky white stuff all over my shoulder?"

Sam knew it was excrement from the startled egret, but she said, "These cypress trees have a lot of white sap on them. Don't touch it. We'll clean it off when we find a safe spot on the swamp floor."

The pair continued jumping from tree to tree for the next twenty minutes. It was now almost dark, and Sam knew they needed to find some dry land quickly while it was still light.

About ten minutes later, Sam spotted a small fishing shack on stilts standing in a small clearing in the swamp. Since there was no land within miles of the shack, it looked like a fairly safe haven for the pair. Without warning, Sam made a leap for the rickety deck that wrapped around the shack.

On the downward side of the leap Portagee screamed out in dismay, "Son of a—" Before he could finish his words, the two went crashing through the old, rotted termite-eaten decking and landed in the murky swamp below. Portagee made his way to the surface. He swam around in circles looking for Sam, but there was no sign of her. What he didn't know was that upon impact Sam's forehead had hit one of the wooden crossbeams holding up the deck. She was out cold before she hit the water. Finally, Portagee dived down into the black swamp water searching frantically for Sam. Without the use of his eyes all he could do was wave his arms around the murky water hoping to bump into Sam. After several attempts, he bumped into Sam's limp body. Portagee grabbed her by the arms and tried to pull her to the surface, but she wouldn't budge. He quickly moved his hands down her legs to discover they were sunk into the muddy bottom up to her knees. Portagee knew Sam would not survive much longer, so he had to act quickly. With all his strength he jerked her left leg out of the mud and then her right leg. As Portagee pulled Sam to the surface, she began to regain consciousness. Not realizing that she was under water, Sam tried to take in a breath. Immediately choking from the swamp water, she began swinging her arms wildly. A second later her head broke the surface of the water, and she gasped for air.

Portagee held her up from sinking back down in the swamp. Finally, Sam calmed down and asked, "What the hell happened? How did we end up in the swamp?"

Portagee replied, "It's a long story, but don't worry. We're all right now." Just then he saw something out of the corner of his eye. He looked up to see a nine-foot gator swimming directly toward them. Portagee yelled out, "Crap, it's a monster gator!" He quickly grabbed Sam by the waist and lifted her as high as he could toward the wooden deck.

Sam grabbed one of the boards and quickly pulled herself onto the deck. She looked back down at Portagee and yelled, "Grab my hand."

Looking back at the gator, Portagee yelled, "No time, Sam!" He reached into his jacket pocket and pulled out a stake he had made to kill vampires.

Sam yelled back, "You can't kill an alligator with that!"

Portagee had no time to respond. Just as the gator was about to clamp his wide-open jaws down on Portagee, he jammed the wooden stake into the gator's mouth. The sharp-pointed stake pierced the roof of the gator's mouth as he clamped down with hundreds of pounds of pressure. The gator's mouth was now stuck open. Not waiting for the gator to snap the stake in two, Portagee quickly grabbed Sam's extended arm and she pulled him up onto the deck.

Both were lying flat on their backs trying to recover from the ordeal when Sam asked, "What the hell happened? I've got one heck of a head-ache." She rubbed her forehead only to find her hand covered with blood.

Portagee rolled over and replied, "Your bloody head struck that crossbeam over there when we crashed through the decking. You were out cold, and I had to pull you out of the mud to get you back to the surface." Looking closer at her head, he said, "Bloody hell! That's one nasty gash on your head. We're going to have to get you some stitches."

Sam smiled and said, "Thanks, Portagee. You saved my life, but don't worry about my head. It will be all right." As she wiped her head again, it was almost healed.

Portagee blurted out, "Holy crap, Sam! For awhile there I was worried that without you, how the hell was I going to get out of this bloody swamp? I guess that's not a problem now." The two laughed as they watched the mammoth gator finally snap the stake in two and swim off into the darkness of the swamp.

Meanwhile back at the plantation, darkness had settled in, creating a host of movement around the grounds. Delphine was one of the first of the blood beasts to walk out onto the front porch of the plantation from inside of the house. As she looked around, she screamed out, "Where is the day walker?"

One of her followers walked around from the side of the house and said, "I slashed all of their tires."

Delphine snapped back, "So where are they?"

The follower replied, "They walked down the road two hours ago."

By now the other vampires were all standing around the front porch. Delphine looked at Duba and said, "Find the day walker and her sidekick and bring them back to me. I will not accept failure this time. Do you understand me?"

Duba replied, "Yes, my queen." He turned to the others and said, "Follow me." Without saying a word, Duba ran down the road with lightning speed. A second later, eight other blood beasts chased after him.

Once down the road, Duba spotted the pair of footprints that appeared to disappear at the edge of the swamp. He quickly turned to one of the vampires and said, "Go now and bring back the chupacabras beasts and get the boats. We'll wait for your return." Duba knew that the swamp chupacabras had been well trained to follow the blood scent of humans.

It wasn't long before Duba and several of the blood beasts were taking the lead on an air boat. The other vampires followed the swamp chupacabras swimming in the water in their pirogue canoes. These canoes were long, narrow flat-bottom boats that were designed to slip into areas in the swamps where the air boats can't maneuver. The vampires were standing up, using long poles to follow the swamp chupacabras as they tracked the blood scent of Portagee and Sam.

Blood Fangs

SAMANTHA SAVAGE
BEAST HUNTRESS

CHAPTER 10

Who's Hunting Whom

WHO'S HUNTING WHOM

Although Portagee and Sam had taken a much-needed rest, they were now making preparations for their beastly visitors. After a couple of hours of working and setting up several surprises, Sam turned to Portagee and said, "When these blood beasts find us, there's no turning back, Portagee. It's destroy the undead beasts or be destroyed."

With a very serious look, Portagee replied, "I'm nervous, but I'm ready." He walked over to Sam, gave her a big hug, and added, "Let's do this!"

Sam gave him a nod and leaped to a very tall cypress tree close by. She quickly climbed as high as she could in the tree, and in the pitch black of the night she relied on her sonar senses as she scanned the swamp for movement.

Portagee climbed up on the flat roof of the old fishing shack and waited for signals from Sam about the approaching vampires. The wait would not be long. The chupacabras were quickly closing in on the blood scent from the pair.

A short time later, Sam began sensing multiple long objects in the water heading in their direction. These were the pirogue canoes being led by the chupacabras, but with all the movement going on in Sam's mind, she failed to detect the air boat with Duba circling behind the canoes. Sam let out a Kiskadee bird call, a bird unique only to Bermuda. Now Portagee knew even in total darkness that the blood beasts were almost on top of them.

Portagee slipped down through a hole in the roof of the old shack. Once inside he dropped down the trap door in the floor, which had been used for fishing from inside. He picked up a couple of buckets of chum he had made up from fish he had caught and a couple of old dead nutria swamp rats he had found in the shack. Portagee knew this foul odor would attract gators, and he hoped it would distract the chupacabras.

The unsuspecting blood beasts were now within twenty yards of the old fishing shack. Sam decided now was a good time to make her move. She leaped at the closest pirogue canoe. Remembering the problem she had landing on the deck of the old shack just before impact, she reached out and grabbed a branch of a cypress tree, breaking her landing. She still hit the front of the canoe with such force that it flipped up ninety degrees in the air. The two blood beasts skyrocketed through the air and landed in the swamp. The canoe was left sticking straight up in the swamp mud. Using the cypress tree branch, Sam flipped back up into the tree. The two blood beasts were left swimming in the water as they tried to make their way to the fishing shack.

Between the chum in the water and the new commotion, the swamp was now teeming with the local gator population. As one blood beast grabbed hold of an old wooden ladder leading up to the deck of the shack, a massive wave swallowed him up. He was gone in a second, leaving a bloody hand and arm still clutching the ladder. A twelve-foot gator had just swallowed the blood beast in one gulp.

The second blood beast and two more from another canoe were now on the deck of the shack. Portagee could hear them from inside the shack and began backing away from the door. He was not very comfortable with his untested weapons, but he had a squirt gun filled with holy water in one hand and a wrist blaster with tiny wooden stakes on the other hand. He pointed both arms at the door and waited. A second later, a blood beast smashed through the door, and to Portagee's relief, the flash grenade he had wired to the door exploded on impact. The grenade made a small explosive sound, but the big event was a massive discharge of ultraviolet light rays that spread out in a 360-degree range. This jolt of light rays created a vampire killing zone of about thirty feet. A blood beast that charged through the doorway was instantly incinerated as he let out a bloodcurdling scream.

The second vampire was a bit more cautious before entering the shack. He slowly peeked into the room, only to find Portagee stumbling around from the disorienting blast and the blinding light. The blood beast jumped at Portagee, catching him off guard. The beast screamed out, "Human! I'm going to rip you to shreds!"

The blood beast now had Portagee by the throat and was just about to rip his throat open. Portagee yelled back, "Not tonight, you blood sucking bastard!" With his left hand, Portagee shot the blood beast twice in the face with his squirt gun.

The blood beast stepped back and wiped his face off. He smiled and said, "You fool, water can't hurt me." Just then his face started steaming and burning.

As he began to flail his arms around, Portagee said, "Welcome to holy water, numb nuts." Then with his right hand, Portagee shoved his wrist over the blood beast's chest where his heart would be and yelled as he fired off one of his mini stakes, "Take this to hell!"

The blood beast gasped and grabbed at his heart as the blood spewed out. As he fell backwards, Portagee tripped the fishing trapdoor open, and the blood beast fell into the swamp to the waiting gators below.

Portagee turned around only to find two more blood beasts waiting for him at the doorway. One of the blood beasts said, "We've been watching you, human, and those toys are not going to work on us." At lightning speed, they moved and were suddenly at either side of Portagee.

Portagee looked around and said, "Holy crap! You bastards are fast." With a pained look on his face, he reached into his pocket and pulled out a flash grenade, and as he dropped it on the floor, he jumped through the fishing hole in the floor. A second later, before the blood beasts could do anything, the grenade exploded, completely filling the small shack with a massive explosion of ultraviolet rays that instantly incinerated both blood beasts.

Back out in the swamp, Sam had just spotted another canoe and instantly leaped for it, but to her surprise, a chupacabras swamp beast leaped at her from another tree, catching her in midair. The chupacabras sunk his large canines into Sam's side. Feeling the extreme pain, Sam's eyes went from blood red to jet black. As they hit the water, Sam ripped the chupacabras off her side by grabbing his tail and bashed it through the canoe that she had tried to land on. The canoe snapped into two pieces and immediately sank. As she tried to pull the chupacabras back to the surface, she felt something tugging on the other end. She found herself being spun in circles under the water. Now she knew what was tugging on the other end of the chupacabras. It was a gator in the act of doing a death roll as he tried to kill his prey. Sam quickly let go of the swamp chupacabras's tail and swam away, only to find herself in the arms of one of the blood beasts who had been knocked out of the canoe.

The beast wrapped his arms around her and said, "Resisting is futile, day walker. Delphine demands your presence."

Sam broke his grip on her and said, "Delphine can go to hell!" As she grabbed him by the arms and flung him into the air she screamed out, "Don't call me a day walker! I'm not one of you bloodsucking bastards." The blood beast landed on his back on an old jagged tree stump sticking out of the swamp. He laid there lifelessly waiting to be gator bait.

She did not even have a minute to rest before something grabbed her long blonde hair. She thought to herself, "Oh hell, it's another gator." Instead it was another blood beast, and out of the corner of her eyes, she could see a chupacabras closing in on her fast from the other direction. Just as the chupacabras was about to strike her, she grabbed him by the midsection and shoved his wide-open mouth onto the blood beast's neck. The chupacabras was now in attack mode and could not be stopped by the blood beast. While the blood beast and the chupacabras fought, Sam looked around for Portagee.

Once the commotion cleared up at the fishing shack, Portagee was left hanging on for dear life to the open trapdoor. One slip and he would become gator bait. Just then, one of the old rusty hinges snapped causing the door to drop more in a diagonal direction. He was now even closer to the water and the gators. While Portagee was trying to get a better grip, the last hinge snapped. Before he could react, someone grabbed him by his jacket collar and jerked him back up to the fish shack. Portagee immediately began firing his squirt gun at the body that pulled him up.

To his surprise, a voice said, "I know I need a bath, but this is crazy."

Portagee looked up to see that it was Sam who had saved him. He smiled and said, "Yeah, you are pretty dirty."

Sam gave him a small shove and said, "You're full of it. Now let's get back out on the deck and see if there are any bloodsuckers left."

No sooner had they stepped out on the deck than two large fishing nets covered each of them. Sam quickly began slicing through them like butter with her sharp fingernails, but before Portagee could do anything, he was swept off the deck. His net was tied to the back of Duba's air boat. Just as the boat was pulling out with Portagee in his net being towed behind, one of the blood beasts lit a stick of dynamite and threw it at the fishing shack.

The dynamite exploded on impact, throwing Sam through the air and skipping across the swamp like a flat rock. By the time Sam regained her wits, the air boat and Portagee were long gone and the only thing left of the fishing shack were four burning wood stilts sticking out of the water. As Sam looked around, a curious gator floated up to her. Sam shook her head in defiance and turned to the gator. With her right fist, she struck the gator's nose as hard as she could. Stunned, the gator simply sank out of sight under the water. Sam, in a very pissed off state after watching Portagee being kidnapped, said, "If any of you other alligators have any ideas, forget it." She looked off into the darkness and stared, knowing exactly where the air boat was going with Portagee—the Black Bayou Swamp Plantation.

Blood Fangs

SAMANTHA SAVAGE
BEAST HUNTRESS

CHAPTER 11

The Queen of Dark

THE QUEEN OF DARK

Duba was racing the airboat at very high speeds through the swamp with no concern for the safety of Portagee. He was still being towed from behind the airboat like a bouncing bobber across the top of the swamp in his fishing net prison. After all, Queen Delphine had shown no concern for the life of Portagee; she really wanted Sam. Duba thought that Sam would try to rescue Portagee. She would not find out until it was too late if he was dead or alive.

Although it was still dark out, Portagee had managed to pull his pocket knife out of his pocket and was attempting to cut through the heavy fish netting. After what seemed to be an eternity, Portagee had cut enough netting and could slip out. Even with the heavy gravitational force being exerted by the speed of the air boat and the constant blinding from splashing water, he thought it was time to try his escape. As he cut one last line in the bottom of the net, his body quickly slipped through the netting. Just when he thought he was clear of the net, his right foot got tangled up in the netting. Now the ride was ten times worse. He was bouncing up and down, continually turning like a gator doing death rolls. At the moment Portagee was about to give up, the netting line simply snapped from all the stress. Portagee went flipping head over heels until his body came to an abrupt stop, landing on a small mass of land in the swamp. As Portagee laid there half conscious, he could hear the air boat's fan blade sound getting fainter and fainter.

It was now getting close to dawn, so even if Duba knew he had lost Portagee there would be no time to return to find him. As Duba pulled alongside the dock back at the plantation, he could see that Delphine had been waiting for him. Duba quickly jumped out of the pilot seat and went back to retrieve the rope only to find it limp in the water. As fast as he could, he started pulling the rope onto the boat only to find the net was empty. He started to turn back to Delphine only to find she was inches away from him already.

Duba tried to talk, but Delphine slapped him across the face and said, "You moron!" She turned to one of the other vampires as she grabbed Duba's arm and said, "Start the fan. It's time you all know I mean business." The vampire did as he was told. Delphine turned back to Duba and said, "This is what happens when you fail your queen." She jerked Duba's arm, and before he could react, she shoved it into the highspeed fan of the air boat. The powerful blades made mincemeat out of his arm. Blood was thrown everywhere, covering everyone in the dock area. Duba screamed in agony. Although Delphine had now pulled him back from the blades of the fan, she was still holding onto his shoulder. She grabbed him by the collar and said, "Do you want me to tie you to the rope and tow you around the swamp as gator bait?"

Duba could barely talk, but he whispered back, "No, my queen."

Delphine threw him out of the boat and onto the dock. She looked at the others and said, "It's almost dawn. Our friends will keep a sharp eye out for the elusive ones, and at sunset we will deal with them." She then walked off in the direction of the plantation with the others following her. Two of the blood beasts helped Duba back to his feet before they followed the others.

Meanwhile, Sam had climbed aboard one of the abandoned pirogue canoes. Instead of leaping from tree to tree, she elected to pole the boat as fast as she could in the direction that the air boat had gone. Sam had navigated her way through the swamp about two miles when the sun's morning rays began filtering through the dense foliage covering the swamp. Not long after that, Sam could see a lone figure waving off in the murky distance. As she got closer, she could see it was Portagee, and a tear came to her eye. She had feared that the blood beasts had already done him in. As the canoe pulled alongside the tiny island Sam said, "I don't recommend this place for hitchhikers." She jumped out of the boat and gave Portagee a big hug. "Are you all right? I was afraid I had lost you."

Portagee laughed and said, "As long as I have my pocket knife, I'm good to go. Those dumb vampires never knew I escaped."

Sam replied, "Well, they do now and I bet they're pissed off. Tonight we'll be on their dinner radar for sure. The question is, do we go back to the plantation now or to New Orleans?"

Portagee snapped back, "I think we should burn the bloody plantation to the ground."

Sam said, "That's good except we don't really know they're in the house. Agent Storm and the Louisiana authorities might not appreciate us burning down a landmark plantation." Sam went on to say, "This wasn't a wasted trip. We still whacked a number of blood beasts that won't be sucking anyone's blood anymore."

Portagee agreed, "You got that right. So can we get the hell out of this bloody swamp and go back to New Orleans?"

Sam replied, "You're right about this being a bloody swamp. Let's get in the canoe and find our way out of this swamp." The two climbed in the canoe and shoved off from the tiny island. Before long, they found a small bayou waterway that led them out of the swamp.

Blood Fangs

SAMANTHA SAVAGE
BEAST HUNTRESS

CHAPTER 12

Storm before the Night

STORM BEFORE THE NIGHT

By late afternoon, Sam and Portagee had finally made their way back to New Orleans. Between hitchhiking, walking, and finally catching a bus, the two arrived back at their hotel.

They went directly to Sam's room first. Just as Sam was about to turn the knob on the door, Portagee grabbed her hand and said, "Wait just a minute, Sammy. Look at that keyway. It's turned sideways. That lock has been picked. I think someone might be in there."

In a quiet voice Sam said, "Well, since its still daylight, it can't be a vampire, and a zombie would be too stupid to pick locks so I think we should go ahead and storm this room." In an instant, she kicked the door open and stepped into the room. To their surprise, agent Storm was sitting in a chair staring out the window.

Portagee was quick to follow Sam into the room. As soon as he saw Storm, he said, "Well, I guess you were right about a Storm in the room, Sam."

Storm stood up from his chair and turned around. His intent was to remain calm and collected, but that approach was not going to work. "Sit down!" he yelled. "Where the hell have you two been for the last two days?"

As Sam and Portagee sat down on the sofa, Sam mumbled, "Oh Lord, he sounds just like my dad."

Storm snapped back, "I heard that. What the hell do you two expect? You've been unaccounted for for two days now. Your rental car was found half submerged in the swamps yesterday. Look at you two; both of you look like shit. Have you been in the New Orleans sewers for two days? You certainly smell like it."

Sam looked at Portagee and then turned back to Storm. "Well, here we go, Storm. Are you really ready to hear this? Oh, if this is not off the record, then I have nothing to say."

Storm was now sitting back down, trying to calm himself. He replied, "All right, it's off the record. What is it?"

Sam went on to say, "Well, to put it bluntly, tonight there will be a lot fewer blood beasts stalking New Orleans."

With a surprised look on his face, Storm said, "You're telling me you've been killing vampires the last two days?"

Sam replied, "You can't kill something that's already dead. You can only destroy the undead."

Storm snapped back, "Oh, that's great. Next you'll be telling me you've destroyed some Voodoo zombies."

Portagee added, "We may have gotten some of them too, sir."

Storm pounded his fist on the end table next to him and yelled out, "Are you two kidding me? This is the United States of America. No one's going to believe vampires exist. Throw in exterminating them and that will be the icing on the cake. When these bodies start showing up, you two are going straight to prison, and the keys will probably be thrown away—"

Portagee interrupted Storm. "They're not going to find any bodies. When you destroy a blood beast they will disintegrate in a few seconds to a few hours at the most."

Storm threw his arms up in the air and said, "You two are going to drive me crazy. Until I see a real vampire, I can't believe your claims."

Sam smiled and said, "Well, that settles it. You can join us tonight in the French Quarter. You'll finally see the blood beasts for what they are."

Storm stood up and said, "All right, where are we going to meet?"

Sam replied, "How about across the street from Queen Delphine's Voodoo shop?"

As Storm walked across the room, he said, "See you there." He left, closing the door behind him.

Sam looked back at Portagee and said, "Well, mate, after tonight Storm will be on our side. With his resources we can put an end to this clan of blood beasts."

Portagee looked at Sam and gave her a nod of agreement, but he wondered how this excursion was going to turn out.

Later that night, Portagee and Sam slowly made their way down Bourbon Street toward Queen Delphine's Voodoo shop. What they didn't know was that they were being watched by Delphine's blood beasts from the dark alleys they passed.

They finally made their way to the street where Delphine's Voodoo shop was. They stood in the shadows across the street from the Voodoo shop waiting for Storm to show up.

As the two stood there waiting, Portagee said, "Where in the bloody hell is Storm?"

Before Portagee could say anything else, Sam leaped straight up in the air and did a back flip, landing right behind a dark figure. She grabbed him by the shoulder and said, "Welcome, Agent Storm. We're glad you could make it."

Storm looked back at Sam and said, "How the hell did you know I was behind you? I didn't make a sound."

Sam smiled and said, "My built-in sonar picked you up as soon as you entered the street. I could tell it was you by the size of the figure I sensed."

Portagee added, "She's right, Agent Storm."

Storm replied, "All right, all right. I might believe you just a little." He looked over across the street and added, "So are you two ready to go visit Queen Delphine?"

Sam looked at the two and said, "Let's go." The three walked across the street, and Storm opened the door to the shop, allowing Sam and Portagee to enter first. The three walked up to the sales counter at the back of the store. Sam tapped impatiently with her longer nails on the glass counter.

A minute later, the curtains in the doorway to the backroom parted and a slender figure stepped out into the light of the room. It was Delphine with her long flowing shiny black hair. She wore an ankle-length blood-red silk dress with slits up both sides that showed her long shapely legs. Storm and Portagee just stood there staring at her. Finally, Delphine said, "Gentlemen and my lady, what can Delphine the Voodoo Queen help you with? Are you here seeking a spell to cast upon someone?"

Sam knew that with her gaga sidekicks she would have to start the conversation. She replied, "No, not tonight, but we have heard of a clan of vampire worshippers who we would like to visit. Can you help us find them?"

Delphine decided to play along with Sam's little game to see where she was going. She replied, "Yes, my dear, they meet nightly at the City of the Dead."

Impatiently Sam said, "Yeah, I know. Been there, done that. Surely you can do better than that."

Delphine was not used to Sam's insolence, but she continued to play along. She asked, "Why, my dear, I don't know what you mean."

Sam stepped closer to the glass counter and leaned over so she was within inches of Delphine's face. With eye-to-eye contact, Sam's eyes went from blue to blood red to jet black. She smiled showing her canine teeth. Sam asked, "Can you now think of anything else to tell us?"

From deep within, Delphine was struggling not to let her vampire emotions explode. She knew that if something happened to Agent Storm while in the shop, the police would be out in full force asking questions. She did not want that. Delphine took her hand and ran her fingers through Sam's hair and gently rubbed her cheek. She replied, "Come back in a few days, and I'll take you there myself for one of their gatherings."

Portagee finally got his voice back and said, "How about during the day?"

Delphine smiled at Portagee. "Are you afraid of the dark? You know that those of us who practice Voodoo believe in zombies. Do you?"

Sam snapped back, "Enough of the small talk. We'll just look around. Can we go see your backroom?"

Delphine replied, "Sure, if you have a search warrant."

Storm was getting a little uncomfortable and said, "Look, we've got to go meet some friends for dinner, so we'd better get going."

Although Sam was pissed, she knew that Delphine was not going to give out any information willingly tonight. Sam turned to the others and said, "All right, let's go." She turned away from Delphine and walked toward the door. Storm and Portagee were quick to follow her. Once outside Sam screamed, "That Voodoo bitch is playing us."

Storm spoke up. "Well, she's playing you anyway, Sam. She got the best of you tonight."

Sam's canines sprung out as she shoved Portagee and Storm aside and stormed back to the Voodoo shop.

Storm yelled out, "You do that, Sammy, and I'll haul your pretty ass off to jail."

Sam stopped in her tracks and turned back to Storm. She yelled, "Don't call me Sammy!" She stomped off in the direction of Portagee and said, "Come on, Portagee. Let's go have a hurricane. I'm thirsty."

Portagee ran after Sam. After all, he had acquired a thirst too.

As Sam and Portagee walked off, Storm stood there wondering what really had just happened. He had seen no sign that Queen Delphine was a vampire. In fact, just the opposite had happened. She seemed the normal one while Sam seemed more erratic in her mannerisms. She was able to leap over twenty feet high, she could turn the color of her eyes from blue to red to black, and she had canine teeth. He decided at any rate that was going to hang around the area and keep an eye out for strange activities.

Blood Fangs

SAMANTHA SAVAGE
BEAST HUNTRESS

CHAPTER 13

The Kidnapping

THE KIDNAPPING

Meanwhile, back in the Voodoo shop Queen Delphine was furious with herself for letting Sam verbally attack her. Delphine screamed out, "Go follow the bitch. Keep me informed of her whereabouts." After four of the blood beasts ran out of the shop, Delphine turned to the others. She said, "We have to find out what this day walker is up to. Or maybe we should just kill her and be done with her. Better yet, I may just turn this blonde bombshell into one of us. She would make a charming princess for me." She turned to the one-armed Duba and said, "Don't worry, Duba. Your arm will grow back soon. Meanwhile, follow that cop and when he leaves the area, capture him. He might be putting two and two together. Take him to the City of the Dead, and once there, to the Crypt of the Undead."

Duba replied, "Yes, my queen." He quickly left the shop with several of his blood beasts.

Sam and Portagee had made their way down Bourbon Street and walked into one of the local bars. Within minutes, they were both sipping on hurricanes. As Portagee took a sip, he looked over at Sam and said, "Sam, you do know these drinks are pretty strong? At the rate you're drinking yours, this night is going to be over quickly. We won't be tracking anyone tonight."

Sam snapped back at Portagee, "Look, mate, you're not my daddy, so ease up." She took a couple large swallows of her drink and said, "I can hold my own." She started to stand up and then abruptly sat back down.

Portagee laughed and said, "I can see you're holding your own just fine right now."

Sam slid the drink away from her and replied, "Shut up!"

Portagee waved the waiter over and said, "Please bring us a couple of strong black coffees." The two sat there planning their next moves.

Storm had never even left the area. With all the activity on the streets at night, he was able to blend in without being noticed. He went into a local pub that Voodoo followers frequented. He sat down on a stool at the bar and ordered a draft beer. While he sat there drinking his beer, he felt something on his shoulder. Storm looked back over his shoulder only to see Duba's scabbed-up bloody stump of an arm.

Duba looked down at Storm and said, "We've been following you. Just looking for the right place to sit down and have a chat with you. Since you're in my favorite Voodoo bar, I don't think any of the local patrons and zombies will mind much if I just kick your ass instead."

Storm replied, "You think?" Before Duba could answer Storm smashed his beer mug against Duba's stub of an arm causing him to scream out in agony. Storm then elbowed Duba in the groin, causing him to bend over in more agony. Storm yelled out, "I'm not done yet." He grabbed Duba by the back of his head and slammed his face on the bar top. The sound of his nose breaking was eerie. Duba was now out cold, lying flat on his back on the pub's floor. Storm stood up for the others and said, "Which one of you bastards is next?"

The three blood beasts stepped backwards, making way for Storm to make an exit. Storm saw the opportunity and decided it was time to leave. He pulled out his pistol and said, "If any of you are thinking about following me, don't!" He slipped his pistol back into its holster and walked toward the back door exit. Storm knew the thugs had entered through the front door and he thought there might be more of them waiting for him.

He thought the back door would be a safer exit. As he walked down the narrow hallway, he noticed the doors to the men's and women's restrooms were directly across from each other. Looking for a last second surprise from the thugs, Storm kept his eyes on the men's room door.

He got a big surprise all right, but not what he was looking for. As he was watching the men's room door, the women's door flew open so fast that Storm never saw it coming. The door hit him so hard, it sent him crashing through the door of the men's room where he laid sprawled on the floor. He never even knew what hit him. A dark figure stepped out into the hallway from the women's restroom. It was Delphine. She looked down at Storm and said, "If you want something done right, then you have to do it yourself." She turned to the other blood beasts and said, "Pick this trash up and get him out of here." She looked over at Duba who was still out on the floor and added, "Leave Duba here. I'll deal with him later." She turned back and left through the back door of the pub, slamming it behind her.

The three blood beasts quickly went over and picked up Storm and carried him out the back door. Duba would not wake up for another twenty minutes.

In the meantime, Sam had sobered up and she and Portagee had left the bar, planning to visit the cemetery again. The walk to the cemetery did not take long. When they arrived at the entrance to the cemetery, Portagee asked, "Are we going back to the crypt of Marie Laveau?"

Sam nodded her head. Then all of the sudden she stopped dead in her tracks. She whispered to Portagee, "I sense the movement of several bodies in the cemetery. I think we should go check that out first."

Portagee replied, "That's fine with me as long as those bodies are above ground and not below ground."

Sam snapped back, "Yeah, right." She then turned to Portagee and said, "Follow me." She took off, zigzagging in and out of the crypts and graves following the sonar images in her head. She already knew she was following mostly blood beasts because their images were lighter and harder to detect since they are already dead. However, she could detect that there was one human traveling with them. She assumed it was a zombie or a human slave. At any rate, they would have to stay well behind the blood beasts as the beasts might detect their blood scent.

Sam and Portagee tracked the blood beasts for about ten minutes through the cemetery. All of the sudden, she stopped dead in her tracks and looked back at Portagee.

Portagee looked at her startled face and said, "What is it, Sammy? You look like you just saw a ghost."

Sam snapped out of it and said, "No, it's just the opposite. They disappeared. I totally lost their images in my mind. It's like they vanished into a wall."

Portagee replied, "Well, maybe they did. Could they have gone into one of the crypts?"

Sam smiled and said, "That's it! Follow me." She turned to walk away and then stopped and looked back at Portagee. "Oh, if you call me Sammy one more time, I'm going to kick your butt." She didn't wait for Portagee to respond. She simply turned and disappeared into the darkness.

Portagee yelled out, "Holy crap! Don't leave me here by myself." He took off running after Sam as fast as he could.

Blood Fangs

SAMANTHA SAVAGE
BEAST HUNTRESS

CHAPTER 14

The Tomb of the Undead

THE TOMB OF THE UNDEAD

Portagee had been right. A hundred yards ahead, the blood beast had entered a two-hundred-year-old crypt. The blood beasts called it the Crypt of the Undead. The first occupant of the crypt had long since been removed from his resting place by Delphine. This large crypt had served Delphine as a place for her blood rituals for years. She also used the crypt as a torcher chamber. She thoroughly enjoyed torchering her victims before devouring their blood.

Delphine had been waiting in the crypt for the blood beasts to show up with detective Storm. The crypt had been modified by Delphine over the years. Since most of the tombs were above ground, she had expanded the crypt tenfold underground. The walls of the chamber were lined with massive oil lamps, which made the chamber very bright. Because of the high water table, every time there was a heavy rain the chamber would flood. This was fine with Delphine because the flood waters washed away the blood and stench that had been created by her blood baths. After the rains there would never be any evidence left behind.

The blood beasts carried Storm down the stone stairs to the lower level of the tomb where Delphine was waiting.

When she saw Storm, she said, "Chain him up to the ship's wheel." The beasts chained him up spread eagle to the ship's wheel. His legs and arms were now spread out at angles. When they had finished, one of them ripped off Storm's shirt.

One of the other blood beasts grabbed the ship's wheel and spun it as hard as he could. He then said, "Copper, that should wake you up."

Storm was starting to come to. His vision was very blurred and the spinning only compounded his attempt to focus. A minute later, Delphine walked up to the ship's wheel and stopped it with Storm in the heads-up position. Storm's vision was focusing quickly now. To his surprise, Delphine was dressed in a skin-tight, almost transparent black silk tee-shirt and stockings. Her perfect figure added to the allure of the moment. Storm could not remember when he had seen such a beautiful woman. As quickly as these thoughts entered his mind, they disappeared. With her right hand, Delphine slapped Storm across the face, digging her claws deep into his skin. She then licked the blood off each of her two-inch-long fingernails.

Storm blurted out in pain, "Delphine, this is the end of the line for you. I'm an FBI agent, and my backup is on his way."

Delphine laughed and said, "You're right, my dear, about this being the end of the line, but it's for you and not me." With her left hand, she squeezed his cheeks and added, "Even if you have backup, they will never find us. If they did, my friends would kill them just like I'm going to kill you."

Storm snapped back, "Go to hell, you bitch!"

Delphine had heard enough of Storm's mouthy remarks. In seconds, she transformed into the blood beast she really was. Storm was shocked at what he saw. He panicked for a minute trying to free himself from the rope bindings.

Delphine asked, "What's the matter, my dear, are you frightened by my inner beauty?" But before Storm could answer, Delphine slashed his chest with both hands, digging her claws deep into his skin. Storm screamed out in agony as the blood oozed out of his multiple wounds.

Delphine was going to go out of her way to keep Storm alive as long as possible. She was not going to bite him until almost the end. She now moved so close to Storm that she rubbed her mouth and face all over his chest, licking up the blood from his wounds. Next, with her index fingernail she slit open his forehead from one side to the other. His forehead began bleeding profusely. She started kissing him as the blood ran down his face and into his mouth.

Delphine whispered into his ear, "I hope you don't bleed to death before the night is over. We're going to have such fun tonight."

Meanwhile, Sam and Portagee were closing in on the area where the blood beasts had vanished. Sam, however, was very unsure which tomb the blood beasts had entered. She looked back at Portagee and asked, "You got any ideas?"

Portagee thought for a minute and said, "Yeah, I'm going to start howling like a wolf, and you keep an eye on those two tombs over there for any sign of movement."

Sam thought Portagee was crazy, but she nodded her head in agreement.

Portagee began to let out the most god-awful howls that one could imagine.

Back in the crypt, Delphine and the other blood beasts could hear Portagee's howling. Delphine was more annoyed by the foul sound of the howling than the howling itself. She looked over at the two blood beasts guarding the entrance and yelled, "Whatever the hell is making that noise, go kill it." The two blood beasts immediately left the chamber.

Outside, Portagee was still howling while Sam laid in hiding on the roof of one of the close-by tombs. A few minutes later, Sam's sonar senses picked up the movement of two faint objects on the ground below. Because of the faintness of the images in her mind, she knew they were vampires. One of the beasts was on a direct path toward Portagee. Portagee was so busy howling he was not aware of the beast's close proximity. Sam could not yell out without alerting the other blood beast, so she just waited for the blood beast moving toward Portagee to show itself. The wait was not long. As the beast rounded the corner of the tomb, both Portagee and Sam saw it at the same moment. The blood beast grabbed Portagee by the throat and lifted him off the ground. Sam instantly leaped toward the blood beast, landing just behind him. She grabbed him by his head and tried to snap his neck in two. To her surprise his head just twisted without breaking the neck.

The beast threw Portagee to the ground and turned his body toward Sam and said, "Sorry, honey, my neck was broken years ago by Delphine. Now you'll have to deal with me."

Sam yelled back at the blood beast, "Don't honey me, you bastard!" She dug the claws of her right hand into his chest and then pushed as hard as she could. The blood beast screamed out in pain as Sam grabbed his heart and shoved it out his backside. As she pulled her arm back out of the beast, she said, "I don't think you can do without this." The blood beast looked down at his beating heart in Sam's hand and collapsed in a heap. His body began to smoke and melted away almost instantly. Sam threw his heart on the ground and pointed in the other direction as she said to Portagee, "If we go that way, I think we'll find Storm."

Portagee was at a loss for words. He nodded his head in agreement and followed Sam. As they made their way to the crypt's open door, the other blood beast was waiting for them.

The blood beast yelled out, "It's your turn to die now!"

With the blood beast's attention focused on Sam, he failed to notice as Portagee spun around behind Sam. As he twisted his body, he now faced the startled blood beast.

The blood beast reached for Portagee and said, "Little man, I'll make a snack out of you; then I'll handle your beautiful friend."

Portagee pulled out his squirt gun and shot the beast in the eyes with his holy water. As the blood beast stepped backwards rubbing his burning eyes, Portagee tripped him. The beast was now flat on his back, and Portagee jumped on his chest and said, "Who's the little man now?" He then shoved a stake through his heart. The beast struggled to pull out the stake, but Portagee refused to loosen his grip on it. A few seconds later, the blood beast was dead. Portagee looked up at Sam and said, "The bigger they are, the harder they fall." He stood up and said, "Are you ready to enter the vampire's lair?"

Sam looked at Portagee and replied, "Yes, ladies first." She stepped through the doorway and vanished in a second. Portagee went running after her as quickly as he could.

Back in the crypt, Delphine continued to inflict severe pain on Storm with the razor-sharp incisions from her claws and by ripping at his skin with her fangs. Delphine paused and turned around when she heard someone running down the stairs. As Sam entered the chamber, Delphine yelled out, "Block the day walker." In seconds, five blood beasts moved in between Delphine and Sam. Portagee entered the chamber seconds later and stopped behind Sam.

Delphine smiled as she stepped away from Storm, licking the blood off her fingers. She looked at Sam and said, "Day walker, your friend is about to join our clan of the undead." Storm was now covered with blood and could barely hold his head up. Delphine stepped back and grabbed Storm's hair, lifting his head up. She smiled as she said, "Your friend will bleed to death in the next few minutes, or maybe I'll turn him in the last seconds of his life. Better yet, if you surrender yourself to me, I'll let your small friend try to save him." With her piercing eyes staring at Sam she said, "What is your choice now, day walker?"

Sam already knew she only had one option and virtually no time. In a split second, she transformed and leaped through the air toward Storm and Delphine. Delphine screamed out, "Wrong choice, bitch!" With lightning speed she turned and dug her fangs deep into Storm's neck. At the same moment, three of the blood beasts leaped into the air, colliding with Sam and knocking her out of the air. Meanwhile, the remaining two blood beasts hit Portagee so fast that he had no idea what hit him.

Sam struggled to free herself from the three blood beasts as Delphine pulled away from Storm, her mouth dripping with blood. As she walked over to Sam, she yelled out, "You're next, princess."

Without warning, Delphine kicked Sam's head so hard she went flying through the air and landed on top of Portagee. Delphine looked at the other blood beast and said, "It's almost dawn. We'll leave our friends a new problem to deal with." With that, she turned and left the crypt, the rest of her blood beasts close behind.

SAMANTHA SAVAGE
BEAST HUNTRESS

CHAPTER 15

A Reality Check

A REALITY CHECK

A few minutes later, Sam and Portagee began to regain their wits and slowly helped each other up off the cold crypt floor. As Sam cleared the cobwebs out of her head, she remembered Storm. Quickly looking over at him, she saw no movement from his bloody body. As she walked toward Storm, she asked, "Is he dead?"

Portagee reached over to touch Storm's neck, hoping to feel a pulse. Just as he placed two fingers on his neck, Storm's head jerked up. His eyes were now as red as the blood that covered most of his body. Storm tried to rip his arms loose from the ropes as he screamed out, "Help me!"

Portagee immediately started untying the ropes. Sam quickly grabbed Portagee's hand, stopping him. Portagee yelled out, "What are you doing, Sam? I'm trying to help him."

Sam screamed back at Portagee, "Look at him! He's turning into a bloody vampire."

Portagee snapped back, "Well, then stop him!"

Sam pulled Portagee back from Storm and said, "There's no stopping the transformation. He's an undead now."

As they both backed away, Storm's transformation was almost complete. Storm could tell what was happening. He let out an agonizing cry and said, "Kill me now before it's too late."

Portagee pulled out a wooden stake from his belt and walked toward Storm, but he stopped dead in his tracks after a few steps. He turned to Sam and said, "I can't do this; Storm's been our friend for years."

Hesitantly, Sam said, "Give it to me." She took the stake from Portagee, but before she could move, Storm snapped the rope bindings and charged at them. The two braced themselves for Storm's deadly attack. Storm threw his body directly at both of them. The impact of his collision with Sam and Portagee knocked both of them to the floor. Storm charged through them like they weren't even there. He ran up the stairs and was out of the chamber in a second.

Portagee yelled out, "Where the bloody hell is he going?"

Sam already knew the answer, but she chose not to tell Portagee. She slowly walked up the stairs with Portagee close behind her. As they reached the entrance to the crypt Portagee also understood what had just happened. Now that it was dawn, the morning rays of the sun had penetrated the city of the dead. Just twenty feet in front of the crypt, there was a large smoking outline of a man etched in the concrete walkway.

Sam dropped to her knees. As tears filled her eyes, she said, "Storm spared us from having to kill him."

Portagee walked over to Sam and bent down to give her a hug. Sam shoved him away as she stood up. Her eyes turned jet black and her fangs were now exposed as she said, "I swear that bitch Delphine and her blood beasts are dead to the world."

A little bolder now, Portagee said, "Look here, Sam." Sam turned around to look at Portagee. He took her by the hand and said, "Come on, let's sit down." They both walked over to the steps that led up to the Crypt of the Undead and sat on the steps.

Sam was first to speak. "Portagee, I don't need a lecture right now."

Portagee replied, "It's not a lecture, but it is a reality check."

Looking a little puzzled, Sam asked, "What the hell do you mean?"

Portagee went on to say, "We just lost a great friend and ally. Now we have no one in New Orleans who's going to help us. We're only going to have these blood beasts trying to kill us, and maybe the police trying to lock us up."

Sam snapped back, "So what? We're both used to having the deck stacked against us."

Portagee added, "Yeah, but this deck is really loaded against us now. Do you realize that down in that chamber we just got our asses kicked? I never knew what hit me, and they were able to stop you dead in your tracks."

Sam set there in silence for a moment and then she said, "Go on, Senor Doom and Gloom."

A little irritated, Portagee went on to say, "Look, we weren't outsmarted; we were out-muscled. Those bastards are tough and deadly. How else do you think they've survived all these years? The only reason we're alive right now is that the sunrise stopped them from finishing us off."

Sam stood up and looked down at Portagee still sitting there. "Well then, get off your bloody ass. We've got things to do today. These blood beasts aren't going to get the best of us anymore."

Portagee jumped up and said, "You go, girl. Let's do it."

As Sam walked down the path, she yelled back to Portagee, "Shut up, you ass!"

SAMANTHA SAVAGE
BEAST HUNTRESS

CHAPTER 16

Hide and Seek

HIDE AND SEEK

The next night back at the plantation, Delphine was waiting for Duba to report what he had found out about the day walker. Delphine was furious. She screamed at the other blood beasts waiting with her in the parlor room, "I had the day walker in my grips. She was defeated, and then the dawn of the day destroyed my victory." She pounded her fist on the nearby table and yelled, "Where is that idiot Duba? I'm tired of waiting. I need to know what's going on." She looked over at one of her servants and said, "Bring me a goblet of blood." The servant quickly brought her the goblet of blood. Delphine drank down the blood like she was drinking a glass of water. The fresh blood seemed to calm her down, and she was now in a more relaxed state. A minute later, Duba entered the room.

Duba's eye twitched when he saw Delphine. His arm had almost grown back, but he was nervous to be in her presence again. As soon as he was sure that Delphine was aware of his presence, he said, "My queen, I have news for you."

Delphine turned and walked over to Duba. "My dear, what news do you bring me? Is it good or bad?"

Duba stepped backwards a couple of steps as he felt a severe pain in his arm.

Delphine saw this and said, "By your reaction, it must not be good news." Her eyes turned fire red, and her fangs were now showing. In a demanding tone, she screamed, "What is the news?"

Duba replied, "My queen, it's not good or bad. It's just news."

Delphine grabbed his good arm and yelled, "Tell me, you idiot!"

Duba went on to say, "My queen, we found the burnt remains of Detective Storm on a pathway in the City of the Dead. There was no trace of the day walker or her sidekick."

Delphine replied, "That's so sad. We could have used a detective in our clan." She shook her head and added, "Nevertheless, take some of our friends back to the crypt and flush out the blood stains before our finest New Orleans police officers come looking for clues."

Duba couldn't wait to leave without losing another arm. He turned to a couple of human slaves and another blood beast and yelled, "Let's go!" The small group left the parlor much quicker than they entered.

Delphine looked at two other blood beasts and said, "You two get out on the streets and see if you can find any trace of the day walker and her friend." The two left without comments while Delphine turned to one of the servants, indicating that she wanted a refill of her goblet.

Meanwhile, Sam and Portagee had moved to a new hotel. They both felt it was best to keep the blood beasts in the dark as to their whereabouts. Portagee looked at Sam from his chair in the hotel room and said, "Well, Sam, you've had twenty-four hours to rethink our game plan. Did you come up with any brilliant ideas?"

Sam smiled and replied, "I'm not sure how brilliant my plan is, but I do have a plan."

Portagee asked, "So give it to me."

Sam snapped back, "All right, all right. First of all, there's too many of them to take on directly like we've been trying to do. Delphine keeps their numbers down based on the available blood supply. Since Hurricane Katrina, the blood beasts' food supply has been so low, Delphine has kept their numbers down to match the supply."

Portagee asked, "Good to know, but what's the plan?"

Sam smiled and said, "We now go into stealth mode. We already know enough of their habits and patterns. We'll start tracking one or two of them at a time each night without them knowing. We might take them out that night or follow them to their lair and finish them off in the early morning dawn hours. This way may take a long time, especially since we don't know their true numbers. Eventually, we'll get our shot at Delphine when she's not guarded by a bloodsucking army."

Portagee thought for a minute and said, "Won't these bloodsuckers pick up my scent when we're following them?"

Sam replied, "You do have a funny smell to you. Just kidding, but you're right. We'll have to stay in contact by our cell phones with you covering my backside from afar. Let's go visit the French Quarter and see if there are any bloodsuckers out for a stroll tonight."

The pair left the hotel and made their way down to Bourbon Street, which was not far away. They had been on Bourbon Street for five minutes when Sam stuck her arm out in front of Portagee, stopping him in his tracks.

Portagee looked at her and said, "What the bloody hell did you do that for?"

Sam whispered back, "Keep still; we're being followed."

Portagee whispered, "Well crap, so much for us tracking the bloodsuckers."

Sam replied, "That's all right. I'm pretty sure it's you they're following."

Portagee whispered back, "Oh great, now I'm the marked man."

Sam added, "Go down that side street right now. I'll have your back, but be prepared to protect yourself if there's too many of them." Sam jumped up to the balcony of one of the nearby buildings. She could sense that there might be two blood beasts following Portagee. They seemed to be focusing on his movements.

Portagee did not say a word. He just rolled his eyes and turned down the dark side street. Just as he walked into the side street, a drunk staggered up to him and said, "Hey buddy, can you spare some cash?" He then leaned on Portagee's shoulder like he was about to pass out.

Portagee gave him a little friendly shove back and said, "Look, mate, go on to one of the shelters and get a good night's sleep."

Portagee stepped to the side to continue, but the drunk grabbed him by the arm and said, "Not tonight! I'm going to get drunk on your blood instead." The blood beast pounded his chest, ripped open his tee-shirt, and leaped at Portagee.

Portagee quickly looked around for Sam, but not seeing her, he yelled out, "Bloody hell!" He reached in his pocket and pulled out a wooden stake.

The blood beast was now directly in front of Portagee, and he just laughed as he grabbed Portagee by the neck and lifted him off his feet. He looked Portagee directly in the eyes and said, "You'll be my dinner before you can use that toy."

With his legs dangling in the air, Portagee reached into the long pocket of his cargo pants and ripped out a Bermuda machete. Without wasting a second, Portagee swung wildly at the blood beast from the side, severing his right arm. The blood beast dropped Portagee to the ground as he screamed in agony and bent over in pain. With another clean swing, Portagee decapitated the blood beast. As his body crashed to the street, Portagee breathlessly said, "Yeah, you're bloody lucky I didn't get a chance to use my toy!"

Before he could say anything more, a voice from behind him said, "Very impressive for a human, but every dog has his day, and yours just ended."

All Portagee could say was, "Oh crap!"

Before Portagee could move, the blood beast leaped at him, but in mid-air he was hit like a ton of bricks and smashed through a nearby store's front glass window. The blood beast stood up with cuts all over his body, looking around for the freight train that just hit him.

Just to his left and out of his line of sight, Portagee heard, "Honey, was I too rough on you? Well then, try this, you bloodsucker!" The blood beast tried to react with speed, but it was too late. Sam had already picked up a large razor-sharp shard of glass and slashed at the blood beast with a leaping spin move.

The blood beast froze for a second believing Sam had missed him. He smiled and started to say something, but before he could, blood began spraying from a massive slice across his neck. Sam leaped back at him and threw a right fist, which struck his forehead. The force of the blow flipped his head back ninety degrees, snapping his neck in two. With blood spewing in all directions, the blood beast collapsed in a pile on the floor.

Portagee walked over to the storefront and checked out the damage. He looked at Sam and said, "I don't think we've got this tracking thing down quite yet."

Sam was still bent over, trying to catch her breath as she looked up at Portagee and replied, "Maybe not, but there's now two fewer bloodsucking bastards in New Orleans." Sam stepped into the street and added as she walked away, "We're done for the night. Let's go get some rest and see if tomorrow we can do any better tracking down these blood beasts." The two left the side street and took an indirect way back to the hotel in hopes that they would not be followed.

SAMANTHA SAVAGE
BEAST HUNTRESS

CHAPTER 17

Tracking the Beasts

TRACKING THE BEASTS

The next night things were different. Portagee and Sam arrived just before dusk in the French Quarter. They were in place and waiting for any blood beasts to pass their way. Sam was keeping an eye on the streets from her perch on the rooftops overlooking the French Quarter. Sam was also using her sonar senses to pick up any traces of the blood beasts. Portagee kept busy working the streets in and around Bourbon Street. He also browsed the local stores and bars for any sign of a blood beast. Every ten to fifteen minutes, Sam and Portagee would call each other on their cell phones. It was a Saturday night, and the streets were crawling with people. Portagee was so short he had no problem losing himself in the crowd. On the other hand, Sam had to rely almost 100 percent on her sharp vision to spot the blood beasts. With so many people on the streets, it was next to impossible to pick up the blood beasts with her sonar due to the fainter image they emitted.

Meanwhile, Portagee spotted what he thought was a blood beast couple. He tried to call Sam, but she didn't answer. After a short walk, he watched the couple enter one of the local bars. Portagee followed them into the bar and found a table out of the way where he could watch them. While he was watching the couple, he tried to call Sam again.

Portagee looked at the cell phone and said, "Bloody hell, Sam, answer the phone."

A second later, a response came. "Bloody hell, Portagee, I am answering the phone. I could see you called, but there must have been interference with the call. So what's up?"

Portagee replied, "I've got a blood beast couple in this bar. I think they're trying to pick up a couple of drunken victims. It's the Cajun Bar not far from where I left you."

Sam replied, "I'll try to find the back door to the bar. See you soon."

By the time Portagee looked up, the couple was making their way to the front door of the bar with the intoxicated pair they had picked up. Portagee thought to himself, "Oh crap, Sam will never find me once I leave the bar." He had no choice. He now stood the chance of losing the blood beasts and of letting two poor tourists get killed at the same time. Once out on the street, Portagee kept his distance as he followed the blood beasts. He knew he could not take the time to call Sam so he turned the GPS app on his phone on, allowing Sam to track him if she thought of it. About four blocks away from the bar, the blood beasts took the tourists into a sleazy hotel. Portagee knew this would be the end of the line for the blood beasts' prey. Once in the hotel, the blood beasts walked right past the front desk clerk. Portagee could see that they had done this before. As they walked up the stairs to go to an upper floor, Portagee was quick to follow. As he walked past the front desk clerk, he pointed toward the stairs and said, "I'm with them." He quickly went up the stairs. The desk clerk pressed a hidden button under the counter as Portagee went out of sight.

Meanwhile, Sam finally made her way to the back of the Cajun Bar. Once inside, she looked for Portagee only to realize he was gone.

Sam blurted out, "Damn it, Portagee. Where the bloody hell did you go? Where are you when I need you?"

A local patron of the bar reached up from his seat, put his hand on Sam's leg, and said, "Baby, if you need a man, I'm here for you."

Surprised and then annoyed, Sam reached down and grabbed his hand, bending it back to a ninety-degree angle and causing the man to drop to his knees. She looked down at him and said, "Mate, if I see a real man, I'll send him to help you out."

In agony, the man said, "What the hell do you mean?"

With her right leg, Sam kicked him in the groin. When he bent over in pain, Sam dropped her free elbow to the back of his head causing him to crack his forehead on the bar floor. As Sam stood back up and walked toward the door, she stopped and replied to the man's question, "Oh, I just thought you could probably use some help since you just got your ass kicked by a girl." The man just lay there as Sam left the bar.

Once she was out in the street, she tried to get a fix on Portagee or the blood beasts, but the street was too crowded and they had been gone too long. Sam went down a side street and leaped to the roof of an adjoining building. She was hoping she would be able to see Portagee from her rooftop perch, but she had no luck. She pulled out her cell phone to try calling Portagee, but she decided that might not be a good idea. If he was still tracking the blood beasts, the cell ring might give away his position. Just as she was about to put away her phone, she saw a blue dot blinking on her phone screen. She then realized that Portagee was sending his GPS tracking signal to her. Sam jumped down to the street and began following his signal.

Back at the hotel, Portagee had followed the blood beasts up to the third floor and was able to see what room they had entered. Portagee knew he couldn't wait for Sam. Actually, he didn't even know if she was following him. He went up to the door, pulled out his squirt gun, cocked his wrist blaster back, and screamed, "Geronimo!" as he charged the door. Before he hit the door with his shoulder the door flung wide open causing Portagee to trip and land on the floor in the middle of the room.

A voice from behind him said, "Well, well, little man. The queen told us to be on the lookout for you. Where's your pretty friend?"

Portagee rolled over on his back and said, "Blow it out your ass." He then fired several shots of holy water into the blood beast's face.

At first, the female blood beast could not be bothered by Portagee. She kept feeding on her victim. When she heard her companion scream in pain, she threw the lifeless body of her victim to the floor and grabbed Portagee by the neck. With both hands on his neck, she picked him up like a rag doll and began swinging him around the room. At one point his feet went crashing through the single window in the room, sending glass out onto the street below.

Sam had just arrived at the hotel in time to see the glass shatter all over the sidewalk. She looked up at the broken window and yelled out, "Portagee, you can't hide from me. I know you're up there." A second later she leaped up and went through the third-story window. As she cleared the window, she grabbed the unsuspecting female blood beast by her head and snapped it off. Portagee fell to the floor and looked up just as the other blood beast was about to recover from the holy war.

Portagee yelled out, "Oh no you don't, you bloodsucking bastard!" With his wrist blaster he fired off three razor-sharp stakes through the blood beast's heart. The beast fell back through the doorway and quickly began to disintegrate like his companion had. Portagee turned back to Sam and said, "Thanks, mate. I couldn't have done it without you."

Sam snapped back, "Thanks for the pat on the back." She looked over at the dead girl on the floor and asked, "Where's her male friend?"

Portagee looked around and then finally opened the closet door only to find him severely beaten up and out cold. Portagee looked at him more closely and said, "He's still alive, and there are no vampire bites on him."

Sam replied, "Thank goodness. Let's get him out of this vampire infested hotel and call 911." Sam picked the unconscious guy up and walked over to the window. Just before she was about to jump, she looked at Portagee and said, "You better get your ass down those stairs before some more of these blood beasts' friends show up." She turned and jumped out the window.

Portagee yelled, "That's right! Leave the little guy here to clean up the mess." Portagee ran out of the room and was out of the hotel in seconds. Sam and Portagee took the young man to one of the nearby hospitals and left him near the emergency room entrance. Sam called 911 to make sure he was found quickly.

For the next several weeks, Sam and Portagee were able to kill off one to three blood beasts almost nightly. Sam's plan was beginning to take a toll on the blood beast clan of New Orleans, but how much longer was the Blood Queen Delphine going to allow this to continue?

Blood Fangs

SAMANTHA SAVAGE
BEAST HUNTRESS

CHAPTER 18

Brothers of New Orleans

BROTHERS OF NEW ORLEANS

While the blood purge of her clan was going on, Delphine had retreated to her safe haven at the Black Bayou Plantation. Tonight she had summoned all of her remaining lieutenants of the clan.

Once everyone was seated in her parlor room, Delphine had her slaves lock all the doors from the outside. She walked to the head of the table and pounded her fist on it over and over. She screamed, "I have never seen anything like this in our three-hundred-year existence! We've got two humans stalking us and keeping us off the streets. One is a day walker, and I would love nothing better than to capture her and find out what makes her different. Her sidekick is a nothing. I wish he was dead or a dinner for one of us."

She walked around the room and added, "We've got to find them and lure them into a trap. I want our slaves out on the streets during the daylight hours looking for them. They must be out in the daylight too." Next, she looked at Duba and said, "This pair is resourceful and smart, but sometimes careless. They can make mistakes. That's when we're going to get them. They're tracking us, and outsmarting us at every corner. So we're going to lead them into a trap and turn the tables on them. Allow a few of our clan to remain on the street so they aren't tipped off. Duba, you make sure we find out where they're staying and then we'll set a trap not far from where their hotel is located. Now leave me alone." Duba and the others left for the night while Delphine invited one of her pretty slaves into the parlor room. Delphine loved the beautiful ones, especially those whose blood she could share. Delphine spent many hours fantasizing about having Sam as her blood slave. After one of her pretty slaves entered the room, she closed the doors for the night.

In the early morning hours after a night of striking out, Sam and Portagee decided to have an early breakfast. The local neighborhood cafe was the perfect place for them to eat in order to stay under the radar with the blood beasts. While they were eating, a large dark figure walked into the cafe. Portagee almost jumped out of his seat thinking it was a blood beast. Sam patted his arm to calm him down and said, "Look outside, Portagee. It's almost dawn. There won't be any blood beasts out at this time in the morning."

The large figure sat down at the table with them. He turned to Sam and asked, "Do you all mind if I join you for breakfast?"

Sam replied, "Not at all. Are you a cop?"

The big man laughed and replied, "You like to be direct, don't you, missy?"

Sam snapped back, "Yes, and don't call me missy unless you want to get your ass kicked."

The big man laughed and said, "No harm done, Sam."

Sam asked again, "So are you a cop? How do you know my name?"

The big man replied, "Well, I'm not exactly a cop—"

Portagee interrupted him. "Oh crap! Here we go playing a guessing game. Come on, mate, it was a simple question."

The big man was no longer smiling. He looked at Portagee and said, "For a little man you sure do have a big ass mouth." He looked back at Sam and continued, "At any rate I do belong to a secret brotherhood that only a few people in the Louisiana government know exists. The name for our brotherhood is Brothers of New Orleans. We were formed at the end of the Civil War by freed slaves. Most white people back then never knew vampires existed, but the slaves of New Orleans were all very familiar with them and suffered and died by them. For over one hundred and fifty years, Brothers of New Orleans has tried to eradicate these vampires from New Orleans, but we are now few in numbers and our enemy still grows stronger."

Sam asked, "So how did you find us?"

The big man replied, "The word on the street of New Orleans is that a huntress is out at night stalking the vampires and killing them. You have killed more vampires in a short period of time than we have in years. Your trail of blood has been easy for us to follow. You might be more careful. The vampires could also follow you. At any rate, that is why I am here. We seem to have the same mission, and Brothers of New Orleans wishes to join you in your crusade. I picked up that your first name is Sam, but not much else."

Sam replied, "That's a noble gesture, but I'm not sure we can accept. Can you tell me how many blood beasts there are in the city?"

The big man replied, "There are probably fifty or more of them. Queen Delphine tries to keep their numbers at a certain level. You know supply and demand. Too many vampires in the city and too many dead people might draw too much attention. This is why New Orleans already has the highest per capita murder rate in the United States. So you are a beast huntress. That is why you call them blood beasts."

Sam looked at the big man and asked, "So how many of you are there to fight the blood beasts?"

The big man answered, "Over the years, we have lost many brothers. With the advent of Hurricane Katrina many of the brotherhood simply gave up and moved away. For several years now, the undead—or, as you call them, blood beasts—have had free reign in New Orleans. We may be few in numbers, but we are committed with our lives." He knew Sam still wanted to know the exact number so he went on to say, "We are now down to just ten in number."

Sam gave him a very serious look and replied, "Let me show you one more thing, then you can tell me if you still want to work with us." She took his hand in hers and stared directly into his eyes. Her eyes went from blue to blood red to jet black. The big man tried to pull away, but Sam held onto his hand and wrist even tighter. She then smiled, showing her small canines while her fingernails grew longer digging into his wrist. Sam asked, "Now do you still think you can work with this beast huntress?" She let go of the man's hand and wrist, waiting for a response.

The big man was shocked and taken back by what he had just witnessed, but he said, "Let me introduce myself. I am Mack, and I belong to Brothers of New Orleans." He looked at Portagee and said, "Yes, most of my friends call me Big Mac." He went on to say, "Now I know why you are so successful in tracking down the blood beasts. Yes, the Brothers of New Orleans is committed more than ever to helping you."

Sam and Portagee both shook his hand and introduced themselves. They spent the next hour drinking coffee and telling each other their background and past history.

Blood Fangs

SAMANTHA SAVAGE
BEAST HUNTRESS

CHAPTER 19

Backed in a Corner

BACKED IN A CORNER

Later that night, Sam and Portagee met with Big Mac and a couple of his brothers not far from Queen Delphine's Voodoo shop. Big Mac went up to Sam and Portagee and said, "These are two of my brothers, Jackson and Spike."

Spike looked at Portagee and said, "I hear you can fire off wooden stakes pretty fast." He then added, "Check what we're packing." He pulled out a stocky pistol and said, "This used to be a 'snake charmer', but we've made some vampire modifications to it—"

Portagee interrupted him. "What the hell is a snake charmer? That pistol looks pretty nasty."

Spike smiled and replied, "Oh yeah. This pistol was designed to fire small shotgun shells. In the swamps, it's the perfect weapon to blow the hell out of water moccasin snakes at close range. My little snake charmer now fires off five four-inch stainless steel spikes one after another. One of these spikes through a vampire's heart is instant death for the bastard it hits."

Sam added, "I'm surprised they don't call you 'bad ass' Spike."

Big Mac chimed in. "So much for introductions. Sam, what's the plan for tonight?"

Sam replied, "I think we should stake out the Voodoo shop tonight and see if we can capture any blood beasts. Maybe we can find out where Delphine's lair is really located."

Big Mac replied, "We haven't ventured into that shop for years. I'll take Spike with me, and we'll keep an eye on the alley entrance. Jackson can go into the shop first while you two wait outside for him. I'm sure the blood beast will spot the two of you quickly, but they'll think Jackson is a customer. We'll keep in touch on the cell phones."

The two groups split up and made their way to the Voodoo shop. Big Mac and Spike hid behind a large trash bin on the opposite side of the dark alley from the Voodoo shop. Portagee and Sam mingled with other tourists as Jackson made his way into the shop.

While Jackson was looking around the shop, one of the shopkeepers walked up to him and asked, "Sir, can I help you find anything?"

Nervously, Jackson replied, "No, I'm just looking."

The shopkeeper asked again, "You must be here for a reason. Come over here, and I'll show you a fantastic love potion." The two walked to the back of the store. The shopkeeper went on, "See, over there on the shelf is the perfect potion for you."

Jackson walked over, picked the bottle up, and looked at it. Before he knew what hit him, the shopkeeper had walked up behind him, and with the speed that only a blood beast could possess, reached into his jacket and pulled out his snake charmer. He fired off one round into Jackson's back. As Jackson fell to the floor, the blood beast said, "You won't be killing any more vampires with this pistol." The blood beast reached down, grabbed Jackson by his collar, and began dragging him into the backroom.

Outside, Portagee and Sam had heard the shot. Portagee turned to Sam and said, "Bloody hell, Jackson didn't wait long to kill the first blood beast tonight."

Sam nodded her head in agreement and added, "Let's go."

The two quickly entered the Voodoo shop and began looking around. They could smell the smoke from Jackson's gun, but there was no sign of him or anyone else. As the two made their way to the back of the store, four blood beasts entered the shop through the front door. One of the blood beasts spoke, "We've been waiting for the two of you to pay us another visit." He quickly pulled out a device from his pocket and pushed the button. In a few seconds, steel hurricane shutters dropped down covering all the windows and sealing the door.

Portagee looked down and saw Jackson's lifeless body along with three more blood beasts standing close to him in the backroom. Portagee looked at Sam and said, "I smell a trap."

Sam snapped back, "Oh really? What gave you that clue?"

The blood beast who had spoken a moment ago replied, "You two are about to die, and all you can do is stand there and argue?"

Portagee answered, "That's not all we can do." He turned sideways and accidently bumped into Sam as he fired off a single shot from his wrist blaster. The stake went off course and struck the blood beast in the forehead.

Sam looked at Portagee and said, "Great shot, ace boy! Now you've gone and pissed him off."

The blood beast stumbled backwards a few steps and then reached up and pulled the stake out of his forehead. He threw the stake down on the floor and with the other three blood beasts began to move toward Sam and Portagee.

Meanwhile, outside in the alley Big Mac and Spike were unaware of the events going on in the Voodoo shop. Big Mac looked at Spike and said, "I don't want to blow their cover, but it's been a long time with no call from anyone."

Spike asked, "Should we call them?"

Big Mac replied, "I think we should just go kick in the damn door."

The two moved from behind the trash bin only to be stopped in their tracks by three snarling chupacabras beasts. Spike looked down at the swamp chupacabras and said, "I hate those little swamp bastards." He reached in his jacket pocket and pulled out his snake charmer. Quickly he fired off three rounds killing the swamp chupacabras instantly.

Big Mac looked at Spike and said, "So much for a surprise entrance." He pulled out his snake charmer and charged the back door to the Voodoo shop. His huge body smashed through the door like it was cardboard. Big Mac crashed to the backroom floor with Spike tripping over him. They were immediately attacked by four blood beasts, who were waiting for them in the backroom. Big Mac fired off two rounds from his snake charmer, instantly killing two of the blood beasts.

Another blood beast leaped through the air, striking Spike in the chest. The blood beast began to maul Spike's chest with his claws. Spike was just able to lift his snake charmer up to the chin of the blood beast and pull the trigger. Covered with blood, Spike threw the blood beast off to the side and said, "I guess you won't be biting anyone else since you just lost your head." Fearing for his life, the fourth blood beast ran out the back door. Big Mac fired a shot at him, but missed.

Meanwhile, in the front of the store Sam and Portagee had their own set of problems. The four blood beasts almost simultaneously leaped over the counters and landed on Sam and Portagee. Three of the blood beasts tried to subdue Sam while the forth blood beast attacked Portagee. Portagee fought valiantly, but lying with his back on the floor, he was no match for the blood beast. He was knocked unconscious as the blood beast banged the back of his head against the old cypress flooring.

Sam found herself pinned down on the floor by the other three blood beasts. The blood beast sitting on her chest yelled out, "Hold this bitch down while I taste her sweet blood." He bent over and sunk his fangs into Sam's neck.

Sam screamed out, "You son of a bitch!" She instantly transformed. In a second, her eyes were jet black. With the strength in her arms, she sent two of the blood beasts flying in other directions. Next, she jerked back the head of the blood beast that was feeding on her. She screamed out again, "You bastard! See how you like this." Sam sank her fangs into the neck of the blood beast, but she did not drink his blood. Instead she made her fangs rip a gaping gash across the throat of the blood beast. Blood spewed straight out like a geyser. She stood up and grabbed the blood beast by the neck, snapping his head off. Before she could turn around the other two blood beasts tackled her from the back.

Sam yelled out, "Oh no you don't, you bloodsuckers!" She flipped over backwards, landing behind the blood beasts. She grabbed them both by their collars and bashed their heads together. Both blood beasts looked up at Sam and were shocked by the sight of blood running down her chin from her mouth. Sam winked and said, "What's the matter, boys? Are you two squeamish at the sight of blood?"

Before either of the blood beasts could answer and before Sam could do anything else, she heard two ear-shattering blasts. The next thing she knew, the two blood beasts she was holding were limp. She dropped them and looked up to see Big Mac standing there with the barrel of his snake charmer smoking.

Sam said, "Thanks, you really know how to use that cannon you call a snake charmer."

With sweat running down his face, Big Mac replied, "I was damn lucky. Not to mention those were my last two rounds."

A second later, Spike walked out of the backroom. Sam started to speak, and then it dawned on her that she hadn't seen Portagee. She quickly looked around and turned back to the other two and said, "Where the bloody hell is Portagee? I haven't seen him since the four blood beasts jumped."

After looking around the room, Big Mac said, "I only see three dead blood beasts. I have a bad feeling that one of them ran off with your little buddy in all the commotion."

Sam banged her fist on one of the counters and yelled, "They're going to turn Portagee into a blood beast like they did Detective Storm."

Big Mac added, "That may be true, Sam, but they took him to get to you. It's you they want. We both know where they took him. He'll be at the Black Bayou Plantation. We'd better get going."

As they walked toward the backdoor, Sam replied, "All right, but you know it's going to be another trap just like this was."

When they made their way out into the alley, Spike stopped and said, "Sam, I couldn't help noticing that you have blood smears all over your face. I thought you weren't a vampire."

Sam looked back at Spike as she wiped the blood from her mouth and said, "Yes, Spike, I might bite, but I promise you I don't swallow." She went on to say, "So much for the small talk. Let's go find my friend Portagee."

SAMANTHA SAVAGE
BEAST HUNTRESS

CHAPTER 20

Lost in the Bayou

LOST IN THE BAYOU

Big Mac had talked Sam out of going into the Black Bayou that night. He felt that they would be better served searching for Portagee in the daylight hours. Sam, Big Mac, and Spike met midmorning and drove out to the edge of the Black Bayou. They met up with a few more brothers who were waiting for them in an air boat.

As Big Mac got out of the car, he turned to Sam and said, "If we drive in, there's only one way in and one way out. With the air boat, we've got options and the advantage of surprise. Also, we might accidently find their hidden lair in the swamp. It might not even be at the plantation."

Sam barely heard anything Big Mac had said. All she could think about was finding Portagee. She walked up to the old rotten dock and after looking at the air boat said, "Are you sure we're all going to fit in that boat? With that big ass fan on the back how are we going to surprise anyone? They're going to hear us coming from the next parish."

Big Mac laughed and said, "This bad boy is powered by a huge V8 Hemi engine, but when we get close, I'll switch it over to battery power. It may not be the fastest boat on the bayou when running on batteries, but it sure can sneak up on gators when we're out hunting at night. Then if it gets too hot, we'll kick the Hemi engine back in and blast our asses out of here."

Sam gave a half smile and said, "Thanks, that's so comforting."

Everyone climbed aboard. It was very tight seating and Sam was a little uncomfortable riding in the air boat. At least it was daylight even in the dark shadows of the swamp. After her ordeal with the blood beast in the swamp, she was hesitant going back into the swamps even if searching for Portagee. The road option seemed much better to her.

Within minutes, the air boat was flying through the outer rings of the swamp. It would not be long before the swamp would become too dense to travel at high speeds. Sam had in her mind that this was going to be a shortcut back to the old plantation. It was anything but that. Two hours later, they were still slicing their way through the swamp with no sign of the plantation.

Finally, Sam looked over at Big Mac and said, "When the bloody hell are we going to get there? I think I could have leaped from tree to tree quicker than this."

Big Mac replied, "Not to worry, Sam. We're not far from the plantation right now."

As the air boat drew closer, Spike noticed through limited openings in the swamp roof that he could see smoke. Spike tapped Big Mac on the shoulder and said, "Look off there above the swamp. I see a massive wall of smoke rising in the distance."

Big Mac replied, "That's not a good sign. There's not much in this swamp that could burn like this. That is, except for the old plantation." Big Mac slowed the air boat down to be on the safe side, but that meant it was taking even longer to get to the plantation.

It was now late afternoon and the air boat was just getting in range of the plantation. Sam could just barely see the plantation, and it was in flames. She yelled out as they drew closer, "I hope the hell Portagee is not in there."

Spike looked at Sam and said, "Well, if he is all we can do is pray for him now."

That was not what Sam wanted to hear. Her eyes went to jet black almost instantly and in an angry voice she said, "I'm not waiting any longer. I can get there much more quickly by leaping through the swamp."

Sam started to leap only to have Big Mac grab her arm at the last second. He pointed off through the swamp and said, "Sam, we've already been spotted. Look through those trees and tell me what you see."

Sam was very annoyed that Big Mac had stopped her, but she stopped and looked anyway. After a few seconds she said, "I see one police officer looking at us through a pair of binoculars and several other police officers now walking up to him with shotguns."

Big Mac replied, "Sam, first of all, remember we're not in New Orleans anymore. We're in the Louisiana swamps in Cajun country." He then added, "Secondly, take a closer look at those police officers. They're local parish deputies, and I'll bet they are on the payroll of Queen Delphine. I think this was a setup, and they've been waiting for us. Oh, and did I mention that they're all white dudes too?"

Spike added, "Now look at us, five black brothers in a boat, and as far as we know, they may think we have Delphine as a hostage in the boat with us. Well, at least they only have shotguns, and we're out of their range—"

Sam interrupted. "I hate to burst the bubble right now, but those cops are sliding boats in the swamp right now. I don't think they're going gator hunting." Before they could respond, Sam leaped from the air boat and quickly scurried up a cypress tree. She looked down at Big Mac and said, "Get your butts out of here. I'll slow them down with a few surprises, and I'll catch up to you later."

Big Mac turned to the others and yelled out, "Let's get the hell out of here." He threw the throttle forward, and the air boat fan created a monster wave that rolled through the swamp. Within seconds, the air boat was almost out of sight.

Three boats full of deputies were not far behind. These deputies were very familiar with the swamp. Almost immediately, they split off in different directions. Even at high speeds, there was no way the air boat was going to get away and elude their pursuers.

Sam targeted the boat that had veered off in a westerly direction. It took her a few minutes to catch up to the boat leaping from tree to tree. Now that she was slightly ahead of them, she grabbed a massive vine overgrown in Spanish moss and swung down on top of them. With her feet, she struck the front of the boat causing it to shift to the left. The Spanish moss flew everywhere, blocking out the pilot's vision of where he was heading. Unfortunately for the occupants in the boat, it was a direct hit with a large cypress tree. The three deputies were all thrown into the swamp and the smashed boat sunk in seconds. Sam never missed her stride and went after the second boat.

Meanwhile, the darkness of the night had settled over the bayou. Big Mac was now very unsure of the way out. He could not turn the overhead searchlights on without giving away his location. The air boat was now almost out of gas. Big Mac finally shut the gas engine down, wanting to save a little gas, and switched to the stealth mode of the electric motor. Although they were running silent, they were still lost. The air boat continued on its tedious journey through the swamps. Two of the brothers now sat in front with their hands out, hoping to see or feel their way through the swamp.

Further back in the swamp, Sam was tracking another one of the boats with her sonar senses. She had to be careful. The deputies were shining searchlights all over the swamp. The lead officer in the boat had his shotgun shouldered and was ready to fire at anything that moved in the swamp.

Sam was now torn by her respect for the law. Even if these deputies were on the take—and she did not really know that—she was hesitant to spill them over in the swamp in the black of night. Their chances of survival would be minimal, given the threat of gators and swamp chupacabras. As they went by her, she dropped from a tree and landed in their boat. Before they had a chance to react, Sam slit the rubber gas line that ran between their five-gallon portable gas container and the engine. With the gas container in hand, she leaped out of the boat, and in a second, there was no track of her.

The deputy with the shotgun said, "What the hell was that?"

The pilot of the boat replied, "I'll be damned if I know, but whatever it was, it just stole our gas." The three knew it was going to be a long night, but there was nothing they could do about it.

Sam left the gas container not far from the stranded boat on a small patch of dry ground. She continued to rely on her sonar senses as she tried to find the third boat before it found Big Mac and the air boat. The wait was not long. Not only did she pick up the last deputies' boat, she also picked up another boat. They were heading straight toward each other. As the second boat image became clearer, it dawned on her who it was. Sam thought to herself, "Holy crap, it's Big Mac and his brothers." Sam leaped down onto the air boat, scaring the hell out of Big Mac and the brothers. Sam turned back to Big Mac and whispered, "Veer left and cut your motor."

Big Mac was confused, but he did exactly as he was told to do. Sam whispered again, "Be quiet now."

No sooner than she said that, the third boat of deputies slowly motored by them. There wasn't more than four feet between their boats. A few minutes later, the other boat was out of earshot.

Big Mac looked at Sam and gave her a big hug. "How in the hell did you do that, little mama?"

Sam smiled and said, "I'll tell you later. Oh, by the way, the other two boats that were chasing us are out of action. Now get us the hell out of here and back to the car before the blood beasts or swamp chupacabras track us down."

Big Mac was slow to answer, but finally he said, "That's a problem."

Sam asked, "Just why is that a problem?"

Big Mac replied, "Because we're lost."

Sam replied, "So does your phone have a GPS tracker app on it?"

Big Mac's voice got much softer now. He replied, "Yes, but in the middle of this swamp, there's no cell signal."

Sam snapped back, "Well, hell then. You pick a direction and I'll guide us with my sonar. Sooner or later we'll come across something."

Big Mac continued the air boat in the same direction they were already going, hoping that with Sam's help, they would find their way out of the swamp. Little did they know that they were really heading deeper into it.

Blood Fangs

SAMANTHA SAVAGE
BEAST HUNTRESS

CHAPTER 21

The River Boat of Death

THE RIVER BOAT OF DEATH

The night was slowly wearing on, and there was no end in sight. The sounds of the swamp were getting more eerie. Everyone on the air boat was now hearing sounds that others weren't hearing. It was evident to Sam that their imaginations were taking over. She only hoped that soon they would find a way out of the swamp.

A short time later, Spike said, "Our battery is almost two-thirds drained. It won't be long before we have to start using the poles to get out of here."

Sam quickly spoke up, "Spike, we may be there. I just picked up a huge object about two hundred yards off to our right."

Big Mac quickly turned the rudder in that direction. He then said, "I hope you're right, Sam. I'm getting mighty hungry. A big plate of red beans and rice would hit the spot right about now."

Big Mac guided the air boat slowly through the swamp. Sam yelled out, "Stop! We're about to run into it."

Spike looked at Sam and said, "I don't see a damn thing. What are you talking about?"

Sam turned to Big Mac and said, "Turn on those searchlights and let's see what's out there."

Big Mac replied, "You got it." He flipped the searchlight switch. The entire area was lit up in front of them. Nobody said a word; they just all sat there staring in disbelief.

Sam was the first to speak up. She said, "How in the hell did that big bloody boat get here?"

Big Mac stayed silent for a while as he checked out the boat from stem to stern. It was an ancient paddle wheel riverboat. The riverboat was huge. It must have been over two hundred feet long and three stories high. The riverboat looked a bit rickety with Spanish moss and vines covering a large portion of it. Finally, Big Mac said, "Sam, that's an old New Orleans riverboat. It's over one hundred and fifty years old."

Sam asked, "How the hell do you know it's that old?"

Big Mac shifted the searchlight further back on the steamboat and said, "See the riverboat's name? It's *The Lafitte*. That old riverboat was thought to have been washed out to sea in a hurricane in the eighteen-sixties. *The Lafitte* and her crew must have tried to escape inland, and I guess they were washed into the swamps."

Sam added, "Well, if this riverboat has been missing since eighteen-sixty, it doesn't speak well for us finding our way out of here."

A bit concerned, Spike said, "Don't you think you should turn those lights out now? There might be zombies and vampires waiting for us on that boat."

Big Mac quickly shut down the lights and after a few moments said, "Look, there's not a light shining anywhere on that riverboat. It's abandoned; it will be safe to go aboard."

Spike looked at the other brothers and said, "Get your ropes ready. When we pull alongside her, we'll tie to the railings."

As Big Mac pulled alongside the riverboat, the surroundings waters became very active. Sam looked down at the water and asked, "What the hell is that?"

Big Mac smiled and said, "That's gators. They're just waiting for one of us to fall in, and then it's dinner time for them."

Sam replied, "Oh, great. We just dropped down another rung on the food chain."

The brothers quickly tied the air boat to the side of the riverboat. As everyone climbed aboard, Big Mac instructed one of the brothers to stay on the air boat. As they carefully walked along the lower deck, Spike stopped and pointed at a porthole. He whispered, "Look, these windows have been painted black. No wonder we didn't see any lights on the riverboat."

An eerie feeling blanketed everyone. Big Mac turned to the others and in a very low tone said, "Brothers, get your snake charmers out and make sure they're fully loaded. We may have stumbled upon the vampire's real lair tonight."

Sam heightened her senses and scanned the area. Afterwards she said, "There's not much of anything going on outside of the riverboat. I guess we're going to have to find a way inside."

Spike replied, "We should go through the engine room at the back of the riverboat. If these creatures are living on this boat then that's probably where they're going to be."

Sam interrupted, "I think we'd better get moving. I'm sensing that there are now swamp chupacabras walking the decks of the boat."

Big Mac added, "They must be using them as watch dogs. Spike, find that engine room quickly." The small group walked as quickly as they could without making any sounds toward the engine room.

The swamp chupacabras were now on the lower deck, and they had the scent of the intruders. They were now making horrible growling sounds. The brother left on the air boat saw them running in his direction. He waited until the last minute before firing his snake charmer, hoping they would not see him. One swamp chupacabras leaped from the riverboat toward the air boat. The brother blew a hole in his head halfway through his midair leap. Before he could fire off another round, he was struck from both sides by the swamp chupacabras. The two swamp chupacabras mauled him with their claws and razor-sharp teeth. The brother managed to fire off one more round, killing one of the swamp chupacabras before the other one ripped his neck open.

Sam and the others heard the shots and the agonizing screams. They wanted to return to help the brother, but they all knew it was too late. Big Mac yelled out, "Run!" They finally made it to the engine room hatch only to find it locked. Big Mac pushed and shoved on the door, but it wouldn't budge an inch. He even pulled out his snake charmer and fired it into the lock with no effect. Big Mac punched the door one more time with his fist and said, "Damn door, what now?" They could hear the swamp chupacabras closing in on them.

Sam finally spoke up and said, "Step aside; I'm pretty damn good at picking locks."

Big Mac snapped back, "We don't have time for that."

As she pushed Big Mac aside, Sam replied, "Oh yes, we do." At almost the same moment, she leaped up a couple of feet in the air and kicked the door with her right leg. The door flung open like it had just been hit by a missile. The others stared at Sam as she ran through the doorway.

A second later, Spike yelled, "Move your butts before it's too late." Big Mac, Spike, and the other two brothers made a dash through the door. Just as quickly as they cleared the doorway, Sam slammed it closed. A second later, the swamp chupacabras were clawing at the door. Big Mac and Spike quickly found an old whisky barrel to jam against the door.

Sam looked at the others and said, "What is that noise I'm hearing?"

Spike replied, "I can't believe it, but the engine in this rusty bucket is still operational. They must be using it to power everything on the boat."

Impatiently, Sam responded, "Let's go find Portagee before those blood-sucking bastards find us." Following her, they quickly navigated their way through the engine room.

Blood Fangs

SAMANTHA SAVAGE
BEAST HUNTRESS

CHAPTER 22

The Hunt Begins

THE HUNT BEGINS

Duba and three of the blood beasts responded to the sounds of the swamp chupacabras. A few minutes later, they found the two dead swamp chupacabras and the dead brother. Duba looked at the dead brother and said, "Well, it looks like we have visitors." He reached down and grabbed the dead brother by his collar and flung him up on the deck. He pointed to one of the blood beasts and said, "Take this human upstairs and we'll have a snack later." Next he reached out and cut the two ropes tying up the air boat with his sharp claws. He then said, "Nobody is leaving *The Lafitte* alive." With his foot, he shoved the air boat, and it slowly drifted away from the riverboat. The other two blood beasts picked up the dead swamp chupacabras and flung them into the swamp. Instantly a feeding frenzy began with the gators ripping the carcasses to pieces. Duba laughed and went on to say, "We have to keep our friends in the swamp alert just in case the humans try to leave our riverboat without our permission."

At the other end of the riverboat, Sam and the others were almost through the engine room. They came up to a door with the word "Galley" painted on it. Sam looked at the others and said, "It looks like our only way out. Are you game?"

Big Mac replied, "Step aside; if it's the ship's galley it can't be a bad room." Little did Big Mac know what he was walking into. Big Mac turned the old rusted knob on the door and opened it. The galley was black as night.

The air was very heavy and had a very foul smell to it. One after another, the small group entered the room. Big Mac turned on his flashlight and cast its beam around the room. At this moment, everyone in the group knew they had found Queen Delphine's lair.

As Sam looked around the galley what she saw almost turned her stomach. There were dried and fresh bloodstains almost everywhere. On one side of the room, three very large butcherblock tables were littered with old human remains and limbs. This must be what they fed the gators and chupacabras. On the other side of the room was an old ice box that must have taken up one-quarter of the room. Sam walked over and opened the door. The sight was worse than she expected. She looked over at Spike and said, "If any of you have queasy stomachs, then stay away."

Spike walked to the door and looked in only to quickly turn his head away. He looked at Sam and asked, "What in the hell are these butchers doing with all these bodies?" The ice box was full of the dead victims of the blood beasts. They were hanging from the ceiling on large meat hooks designed to hang sides of beef.

Sam pulled Spike away, closed the door, and said, "These bloodsuckers keep the bodies fresh in the icebox and feed on them at their leisure." Sam couldn't help but look around to make sure Portagee was not hanging from a hook. To her relief, she did not see him.

Big Mac walked up with his snake charmer in one hand and said, "We're going to kill every one of these bloodsucking bastards tonight. It ends here tonight!"

Sam replied, "First we find Portagee; then we kill Delphine. After that, we can wipe out this hellhole. Now let's get moving." As they entered the next room, Sam asked, "Where the hell are we now? I don't think I even want to know what that huge tank is used for."

Big Mac replied, "Not to worry. We're in the boiler room now, and that tank is where the steam was created to power this river boat. If this baby ever blew anything in this section of the swamp would be blown to pieces."

Sam asked, "Are you telling me this one-hundred-fifty-year-old contraption is still working?"

Big Mac replied, "Yep. That must be how they're getting their power out here in the middle of the swamp. There's tons of wood to burn out here."

Spike walked over to the next door, pulled out his snake charmer, and said, "Let's check out this room."

Meanwhile, Duba had made his way back to the top deck of the riverboat. The center room on this deck was Delphine's hidden throne room. As he entered the room, he said, "We have visitors on the lower deck, my queen."

Delphine stood up from her throne and said, "Is it the day walker looking for her little friend?"

Dubba replied, "I did not see or hear her, but the chupacabras killed one of the Brothers of New Orleans." He then had one of the other blood beasts throw his body down in front of her. He went on to say, "I cut their boat loose and left one guard on the lower level to look for them."

Delphine walked over to the dead brother and picked up his body. Then she dropped it on the long wooden, marble-topped table. She waved to the others to join her and turned back to Dubba. "Take several of the guards. Find and kill whomever you see, unless it's the day walker."

Duba replied, "Yes, my queen." He snapped his fingers and four other blood beasts left the room with him.

The next room Sam and the brothers entered appeared to be a waiting room. Sam looked around and said, "This must be where the guests of Queen Delphine wait to be announced or to die—"

Spike interrupted her. "We've now been in every room on this level of the riverboat. Why are we wasting time? We know the bloodsuckers must be on one or both of the upper levels."

Sam snapped back, "You're right. Let's gear this up a notch." She looked around quickly. As soon as she saw the stairway leading up to the next level, she said, "Try to keep up with me now."

From the base of the stairs, she leaped up to the next level and vanished into the darkness. Almost as soon as she cleared the stairway, a sliding steel door sealed off the stairway. Sam was on one side of the door and the Brothers of New Orleans on the other.

Blood Fangs

SAMANTHA SAVAGE
BEAST HUNTRESS

CHAPTER 23

Divide and Conquer

DIVIDE AND CONQUER

All the brothers were stunned. They each just stood there waiting for someone to say the first word. Finally, Big Mac spoke up. "The Brotherhood of New Orleans has waited for over one hundred fifty years for a chance like this to wipe out this clan. That damn steel door is not going to stop us. We'll go back outside and take those stairs to the upper two levels. Let's go!" Big Mac walked over to an outer door hatch with his snake charmer in one hand. With his other arm, he smashed the hatch. The hatch door blew off its hinges and slid across the deck and into the water. He stepped out onto the deck and made his way to the outer stairway with his brothers close behind him.

Meanwhile, by the time Sam had landed on the upper deck floor, the door had already slid closed. She walked back to the door and tried to slide it open, but to no avail. She knew not to yell for Big Mac and the others because she sensed that someone might be watching her. This level of the riverboat had so many walls in it that her sonar sensing was of very little help. All she knew for sure was that she was at the front of the riverboat and there would probably be more than fifty rooms to check. The deck appeared to have two parallel hallways running from one end of the riverboat to the other. As Sam started to walk down the hallway on the right, she could hear a snarling, growling sound closing in on her very quickly. She thought to herself, "Oh crap! If that sound is from swamp chupacabras, this is going to get nasty." In the long hallway, her sonar senses could now pick those beastly little bastards up. At the last second before they jumped at her, she leaped and grabbed an oil lamp light fixture hanging from the ceiling. Just when she thought she was safe, the rusty old fixture snapped off its base sending Sam crashing to the floor. The two chupacabras abruptly stopped and turned to attack Sam. Before she knew what hit her, the two beasts were crawling all over her, clawing and biting her with their massive fangs. In excruciating pain, Sam grabbed one of the scaly beasts by his neck. She dug her long nails as deep as she could and beat him against the wall and the floor as fast as she could. Before she could let go of the beast, the other beast leaped at her, digging his fangs deep into her neck. The beast was going for the kill. Sam could not waste a second. She threw down the dead chupacabras she was holding and grabbed the other chupacabras with both hands. She grabbed him by the snout and slowly pulled the fangs out of her neck. Blood was now flowing profusely from her neck. She had very little time to kill the chupacabras and save herself. Sam ripped open his jaws, splitting his skull in half. Sam quickly ripped one of her sleeves off her blouse, wrapped it around her neck, and tied it off. She knew if she could stop the bleeding for a few minutes, her body would start to heal itself very quickly.

As she stood up to move on a voice from the darkness said, "Why did you wrap up that wound? I was hoping to taste some of that vixen blood."

Sam knew it was a blood beast speaking. Her eyes went jet black as she said, "Jackass, that's not going to happen in your life."

The blood beast laughed and said, "I'm already dead, you bitch."

Sam was pissed now. She bounced off the wall beside the blood beast and landed behind him. She whispered into his ear, "You're nothing but a heartless bastard." She shoved her hand through his back and in an instant ripped his heart out from his backside. The blood beast dropped to his knees and then fell forward on his face. Sam threw his black, smoldering heart on the floor and stomped on it. She looked down at the dead blood beast and said, "See, I told you it was never going to happen." Sam felt her neck. It had almost stopped bleeding. The first several rooms she looked into were not occupied, but she could now tell that these rooms must be the daytime resting places for the blood beasts. This riverboat had to be destroyed.

The brothers were now on the outer deck on the same level. Spike and Big Mac were walking side by side with the other two brothers following a few feet behind them. Two blood beasts jumped out of a hallway and immediately attacked Spike and Big Mac. Another blood beast swung down from the upper deck and wrapped his legs around one of the other brothers, swinging him off the deck dropping him into the swamp below. Within seconds, all you could hear was splashing and screaming in the swampwaters below. The brother was ripped to shreds in seconds by the gators.

The blood beast that attacked Big Mac had his mouth wide open with his fangs showing. Big Mac looked at the blood beast and yelled, "You want a piece of this?" He shoved his snake charmer into the wide open mouth of the blood beast and yelled, "Bite this, you bloodsucker." A second later, he pulled the trigger on the snake charmer, blowing the back half of the blood beast's head off.

Spike looked over at Big Mac and said, "Damn, brother, you're good." Before he could say anything else, the other blood beast grabbed Spike by the arm and bit him. Spike yelled out in pain, but before he could react, the blood beast flung him over the side of the deck. Big Mac quickly shot the blood beast through the heart with his snake charmer.

Spike was lucky, if you could call falling to the hard wooden deck below lucky. His head and arms were hanging over the side of the deck. Just as he was getting his wits back, a gator leaped from the swamp directly at his head. Spike quickly fired off two rounds from his snake charmer into the head of the gator. The gator did a belly flop in the swampwater and sank from sight.

Back on the deck above Spike, Big Mac leaned over the rail and yelled out, "Brother, are you still alive? Can you hear me?"

Spike yelled back, "Hell yes, you big dumb bastard! It's going to take more than a blood beast and a gator to kill me."

Big Mac snapped back, "Well then, get your ass back up here. I don't know what the hell you were doing down there anyway."

Sam had heard the shots from outside on the deck. She assumed the brothers were on the attack, so she kept up her searching. As she checked more rooms, she couldn't help but think she might not find Portagee alive. Sam was at the last door in the hallway. Having found no sign of Portagee, she was a little careless opening this last door. She pushed it open with her left hand and quickly stuck her head into the room. No sooner had she done that the door came right back at her striking her in the forehead. She flew back across the hallway crashing through the door on the other side of the hall. Sam was dazed and before she could regain her senses, a blood beast grabbed her by the feet and dragged her back out into the hallway. Two blood beasts picked her up by her collar and started banging her head against the walls in the hallway. Sam's face was now covered with blood and just at the moment her knees were about to buckle, one of the blood beasts lifted her back up and threw her down the hallway. She crashed headfirst into the steel stairway that led upstairs. Sam was now out cold. They could have left her for dead. One of the blood beasts could not contain himself after seeing Sam covered with blood. He walked over to her and rolled her over on the stairs and straddled her. He then shoved her head to one side and sunk his fangs deep into her neck and began gorging himself with her blood.

A few seconds later, someone grabbed the blood beast's hair and jerked his head up off Sam's neck. The voice screamed out, "I told you she was mine; now bring her to me!" Next a swishing sound ripped through the air and the blood beast's head went flying through the air. Queen Delphine snapped at the others, "Bring the day walker to my chamber. Then go kill the rest of the intruders." Delphine went back to her chamber with her prisoner.

Blood Farms

SAMANTHA SAVAGE
BEAST HUNTRESS

CHAPTER 24

The Big Mac Attack

THE BIG MAC ATTACK

Big Mac finally made his way onto the second floor of the riverboat. Sam's trail of dead chupacabras and blood beasts was not hard to follow. When they came to the end of the hall and found the decapitated blood beast, Spike said, "Look, Big Mac, this isn't the work of Sam. I've never seen her use a weapon like a sword before. It looks like another blood beast did this to his fellow bloodsucker."

Big Mac asked, "Why the hell would he have done that to one of his own?"

Spike looked around and said, "Look, there's blood wall to wall here, and I'll bet it's Sam's blood. I think she got the hell kicked out of her by an ambush. This bloodsucking bastard must have tried to kill her, and instead he got the wrong end of the stick by someone."

Big Mac said, "Brothers, we know she's upstairs somewhere. All we have to do is go find her and kill the rest of those bastards."

Spike asked, "How in the hell are we going to find them?"

Big Mac pointed to the floor and the blood droplets and then replied, "Let's start with the blood drops on the floor. We'll follow them." He turned back to the others, adding, "Reload those snake charmers and keep some extra ammo in your pockets. This is going to get messy. Now let's go and get Sam and Portagee back." One behind the other they quietly went up the stairway.

Just as Spike reached the top stair, three blood beasts charged out of the darkness. They hit the brothers with such speed that the brothers never got a single shot off. All six of them went rolling down the stairs. Spike found himself flat on his back with a blood beast slicing through his skin like it was paper. The blood beast protruded his fangs and went for Spike's neck.

Spike yelled out, "You're not biting me, you bloodsucking bastard!" Spike reached up with one hand and grabbed the blood beast by the hair on his head. With his other hand, he shoved the snake charmer just under his chin. As he squeezed the trigger, he screamed, "Suck on this!" Spike's shot blew off the back half of the blood beast's skull.

The two other blood beasts disappeared into the darkness once the snake charmer was fired.

Big Mac helped Spike to his feet. As they looked around, they saw the lifeless body of one of their brothers. By the way he was lying on the deck, it was obvious his neck was broken.

Spike lifted him up slightly from the deck and hugged him. He screamed out, "They will pay for this." He laid him back down on the deck and flipped open the chamber of his snake charmer. He ejected the spent shell and replaced the empty chamber with a fresh bullet. As he snapped the chamber closed, he said, "Every shot counts with these bloodsuckers, and there's no way I want to be one shot short."

Big Mac and Spike quickly looked around and then slowly made their way back up the stairs.

Meanwhile, on the upper level in Delphine's hidden chamber, Sam came to only to find she was chained to a wall. The room was dimly lit and Sam could not see much, but she did sense another's presence. Sam whispered out, "Portagee, is that you?"

A voice from the darkness rang out, "Hell no, you bitch! At this moment your little friend is being dropped overboard to become gator bait."

Queen Delphine stepped out of the darkness then so Sam could see her. Sam lifted her head and jerked at the chains as hard as she could. She yelled out, "Free me, you bloodsucker, and I'll rip you to shreds."

Holding a three-foot buggy whip, Delphine walked over to her. The leather strap on the end was about six inches long. She passed the whip slowly across Sam's face and then across her chest. Without warning, Delphine snapped the whip across one side of Sam's face and then the other side. Blood ran down Sam's face. Delphine wiped her fingers in it, and then she placed her fingers on her lips and licked the blood. Delphine smiled and said, "Your blood is sweet. I'm not sure I can control myself with you."

Sam's eyes were now jet black and her small canines were showing. She shook her head and said, "Enjoy yourself now because when I free myself, you'll be the one swimming with the gators."

Delphine glared at Sam as she whipped her several more times. She grabbed Sam by her hair and jerked her head back. With her tongue, she licked more blood from Sam's face. Within inches of Sam's face, she whispered into her ear. "What are you? You have the eyes, the fangs, and the claws of a vampire, but you don't taste like one or even act like one. You don't even drink blood, do you, my love?"

Sam showed her teeth and said, "I may make an exception with you."

Not frightened by Sam's threat, Delphine said, "Oh, I like that idea, my lovely." She gripped Sam's chin with one hand. "You heal slowly for a vampire, but I see you are healing, day walker."

Sam spit at Delphine and said, "I'm not a day walker, you bitch."

Delphine was pissed now. She stomped her foot and slapped Sam as hard as she could. Then she grabbed Sam by the hair and bent her head back as far as it would bend without breaking her neck. Delphine's eyes were jet black and her fangs were fully extended. She yelled, "I'm through with you! Tonight I'm going to turn you, and you'll be my slave for eternity." She lunged at Sam and put a death grip on her as she sank her fangs deep into Sam's neck.

Sam screamed out in pain as she tried to free herself, but to no avail. Her eyes looked like mini-hurricanes as they swirled from red to black to white. A minute later, she blacked out as Delphine kept feeding on her blood. Finally, Delphine stopped. She threw Sam's limp body on the floor and walked away, wiping the blood from her mouth. She quickly left the chamber to check on the other intruders.

Meanwhile, Duba and two other blood beasts had Portagee hanging by his feet from an old cargo crane off the side of the riverboat. They had been slowly lowering Portagee down to the swamp below. He was now about five feet above the swamp and the local gator population had taken notice. Several of the gators were now leaping at Portagee's head.

One deck below, Big Mac and Spike had seen Portagee's predicament. In a low tone, Big Mac said, "You go back down and try to swing Portagee back to the riverboat while I go upstairs and kick some vampire ass." The two went in opposite directions.

Spike was quick to reach the bottom deck. He yelled out, "Portagee, swing this direction and I'll catch you."

Portagee was shocked to see Spike and yelled back, "You got that." He quickly began swinging toward Spike.

Backup on the top deck, Duba could see what was going on. He yelled out, "Cut that damn rope." The blood beast flipped out his six-inch switchblade and then grabbed the rope with his other hand.

Before he could cut the rope a, voice rang out, "Not tonight you're not." A loud bang rang out. The blood beast was struck in the back. The force of the shot sent him flying over the rail of the upper deck. A second later, he was being devoured by the gators in the swamp. Another blood beast reached out for the rope only to have his hand blown off from another shot fired by Big Mac. Big Mac stepped out of the darkness to fire another shot, but before he could, Duba jumped up on the railing and swung his machete slicing through the rope like it was butter.

In the middle of his swing, Portagee dropped so quickly that Spike let him slip through his arms. Reacting instinctively, he tried to grab the rope. As the rope slipped through his hands, Spike ignored the sting of the rope burning his skin. Finally, he got a full grip on the rope, but not before Portagee splashed down in the swamp. With all his might, Spike jerked Portagee back out of the swamp. He was able to pull Portagee half-way over the railing of the riverboat and then he noticed Portagee was not alone. There was a five-foot gator hanging onto his shirt collar.

Portagee screamed out, "Get this bloody creature off me!"

Spike was struggling to hang onto the rope with one hand while he pulled out his snake charmer with the other hand. Finally, he got the snake charmer out and fired it at the side of the gator. The gator let go of Portagee and dropped back into the swamp. Spike quickly pulled Portagee onto the deck and began untying his feet.

Back on the top deck, Duba looked back around to see that Big Mac had his snake charmer trained on him. Big Mac said, "Say goodbye, bloodsucker." He fired the snake charmer, but Duba vanished before the slug left the barrel. Big Mac looked around in disgust.

Duba had survived for hundreds of years and there was no way he was going to let Big Mac get the drop on him. He leaped off the upper deck and swung down to the lower deck. He flew over the top of Portagee and collided with Spike, knocking him against a wall. A second later, Duba had vanished again. As Portagee got to his feet, he looked over in the darkness and saw Spike's outline against the riverboat wall. He said, "Spike, are you OK?" He did not get an answer from Spike. As he walked closer, he discovered the reason why. Spike had been impaled through the chest with Duba's machete. He had died instantly. Big Mac ran down the outer stairway just seconds behind Portagee. He saw Spike's lifeless body hanging on the wall. He dropped to his knees and cried. The big man had lost his best friend, and he was not going to forget which blood beast had done this. He reached up and removed the machete from Spike and then laid him down on the ship's deck. He would come back later to recover his body.

SAMANTHA SAVAGE
BEAST HUNTRESS

CHAPTER 25

The Transformation

THE TRANSFORMATION

Sam was sprawled out on the floor in a pool of her own blood. The chains on her wrists and waist still held her captive. Muscle impulses were beginning to run through Sam's body. At first she was relieved to feel movement in her body, but that sensation did not last long. As she moved around shooting pains ripped through her body. She could now feel the bone-chilling cold blood flowing throughout her body. As the blood pumped through her heart, it felt like her chest was going to explode. In excruciating pain, Sam stood up and let out a bloodcurdling scream.

Seconds later four blood beasts rushed into the chamber. The first blood beast to enter the room pointed at Sam and laughed. "Look, the day walker is joining our clan. She's becoming one of us."

Sam slowly lifted her head up and then her eyelids snapped open. All of the sudden, the blood beasts quit laughing. The irises of Sam's eyes were jet black and the pupils of her eyes were blood red. Sam screamed out, "I'm not a day walker, you bloodsuckers!" With all her might she ripped at the chains, snapping them off from the steel U-bolts that were holding them to the wall. With her waist and arms free, she began snapping the chains overhead like whips. Whipping both chains with newfound strength, she snapped them at the same time, wrapping them around the necks of two of the blood beasts. She jerked both chains back toward her with such force that both blood beasts were decapitated. The other two turned to run back out the door only to find Big Mac and Portagee waiting for them. One of the blood beasts ran into Portagee and got a wooden stake driven through his heart while the other blood beast was shot through his heart with Big Mac's snake charmer.

Portagee walked into the room while Sam was breaking the chains from her wrists. Portagee looked at her eyes and the new reddish streaks in her long blonde hair. "I like your new look, Sam." He then walked over and gave her a big hug and added, "Are you all right?"

Sam let go of Portagee and replied, "I'm not sure. I've been bitten by blood beasts before, but Queen Delphine is the most powerful blood beast that has ever sank her fangs in me. She drank so much of my blood I blacked out."

Portagee added, "As soon as you get a craving, let me know what it's for—hamburgers or me."

Sam looked over at Big Mac and asked, "Where's Spike and the others?"

Big Mac replied in a low tone, "We've lost our brothers tonight." He went on to say, "We're not leaving this riverboat of death until the clan is destroyed."

Portagee added, "Well, let's put it this way, this is the lair of the blood beasts. It's either them or us. If the blood beasts have their way, we'll be the ones destroyed tonight.

Sam walked toward the door and said, "Let's go finish these blood beasts off before they take us out." She walked through the door and was out of sight in a second. Portagee and Big Mac took the hint and ran after her.

Blood Fangs

SAMANTHA SAVAGE
BEAST HUNTRESS

CHAPTER 26

The Fires of Hell

THE FIRES OF HELL

Down on the lower deck, Duba found Delphine and other blood beasts in the ship's galley. Delphine looked at Duba as he entered the galley and asked, "Did you destroy the humans?"

Duba knew he would have to be very careful with his answer. So he chose his words very carefully. He replied, "My queen, we have eliminated three of the humans. There are still two onboard alive."

Delphine asked, "Then why in the hell are you here? Where are the humans you already killed? We are hungry for their blood."

Duba knew where this conversation was going, and he knew it was not going to go in his favor from this point on. Duba went on to say, "My queen, two of the humans were lost overboard and were devoured by the gators and the chupacabras. The third human I impaled on the wall just before arriving. These humans were from the Brothers of New Orleans. I thought we had killed them all off."

Delphine snapped her fingers and said to two other blood beasts, "Bring that human back to the galley." The two blood beasts immediately left the room. Delphine turned back to Duba and added, "That's what you get for thinking. Are these other two humans Brothers also?"

Duba responded, "Yes, one is called 'Big Mac' and the other one is the day walker's sidekick. The Brothers helped him escape before we could feed him to the gators." Duba went on to ask, "Where is the day walker?"

With lightening speed, Delphine threw her body into Duba and knocked him flat on the floor. She stood over him with one of her sharp stilettos pressing hard against his chest. With a piercing look, she said, "Say the wrong thing, Duba, and I'll shove my heel through your heart. Do you understand me, you idiot?"

Undergoing an intense amount of chest pain, Duba replied, "Yes, my queen."

Delphine went on to say, "Don't worry about the day walker. I've turned her into one of our clan. She's chained up in my chamber and won't be a problem. But the other two humans must be eliminated before dawn. I want to sleep in peace in the morning." She pushed her heel a little harder in Duba's chest and said, "Do you understand?"

Duba could hardly breathe now. He squeaked out a reply, "I will take care of the humans."

Delphine removed her heel from Duba's chest and yelled, "Good! Now take whom you need and get the hell out of my sight."

Duba jumped up without saying a word. He signaled for several blood beasts to follow him. They all quickly departed from the galley.

Meanwhile, Portagee and Big Mac caught up with Sam at the opposite end of the upper deck. Big Mac was the first to speak. He said, "The blood-suckers are below. Why aren't we going down after them?"

Sam still stood there in silence. Still worried about Sam, Portagee asked, "Are you sure you're all right?"

Sam responded, "Right now I've got a million things going on in my head. It's hard to keep focused." She looked at Big Mac and said, "I'm sorry for not answering, but I was just thinking that it's just a few hours before dawn. These blood beasts must be getting nervous that we're still on their riverboat. Once dawn comes, the advantage will be ours—if we can survive that long. There might be one problem however."

Portagee asked, "What's that?"

Sam replied, "After the bite I took from Delphine, I'm not sure how I'll react." She went on to say, "Because all the riverboat's windows are painted black, even in the daylight we'll still have to go in after them."

Big Mac replied, "Yeah, and since this is their turf, they'll be waiting for us—"

Sam interrupted, "I've got good news and bad news for you. The good news is that my sonar senses are still working, but the bad news is that there are five blood beasts coming up the stairs from the lower level right now."

Big Mac pulled out his snake charmer and cocked the trigger back. "I've got five shots in this old charmer. That's just enough to get the job done."

Portagee replied, "I don't like those odds, especially since some of them seem to be able to move quicker than we can see them. Maybe if we had an AK-47, it would be more equal."

Sam was getting impatient. She said in a low tone, "Enough of the small talk, boys. I'm going to leap over to that cypress tree and distract them. Big Mac, you unload your snake charmer on them from the top of the stairway." She smiled as she looked at Portagee and said, "Portagee, you finish them off with your squirt gun." A second later, she leaped to the cypress tree that was about twenty yards out in the swamp.

Big Mac looked at Portagee, who was stuttering in an attempt to find his voice. Finally, he said, "She said what with a squirt gun?"

Portagee replied, "Don't worry about it. Just get your bloody butt going." The two ran to the stairway entrance on the top deck and waited.

Sam watched as the blood beasts made their way up the staircases. When they were about halfway up the last set of steps, Sam made her leap toward the riverboat. Just as she was about to land she yelled out, "Die, you bloodsucker!"

The blood beasts froze in their tracks, looking at Sam. Big Mac jumped out from the shadows and fired off all five rounds as fast as he could. As the smoke from his snake charmer was clearing Big Mac yelled out, "Now that's what I call kicking ass."

A second later a blood beast jumped through the smoke and hit Big Mac with such an impact that he fell flat on his back. The blood beast was now sitting on Big Mac's chest. His claws were fully extended and just as he was about to slice open Big Mac's chest, water came flying through the air. The blood beast's face began smoking and burning. He jumped up grabbing at his face and fell over the rail into the swamp. Within seconds, he was being ripped to pieces by the gators. As Big Mac began to sit up, he heard a voice say, "Now, big man, you know what a squirt gun filled with holy water can do."

Just then another figure stepped through the smoke. Portagee caught the movement out of the corner of his eyes and spun around, firing off his squirt gun in rapid succession. A voice yelled out, "Portagee, what in the bloody hell are you doing? I don't need a bath."

Portagee could now see he had just soaked Sam's face with holy water. He stood there and stared at Sam.

Wiping the water from her face, Sam said, "So what are you staring at?"

Portagee replied, "I'm sorry, Sam, but I was scared that your face was going to ignite in flames."

Sam walked up to Portagee and gave him a hug. She said, "Thanks, but get over it. I'm not a freaking blood beast." She smiled and added, "However, I may be too hot to handle."

As Big Mac got back to his feet, he asked, "How many blood beasts did I blow away?"

Sam answered, "It was a good effort, big man, but you only took out two of them."

Portagee yelled out, "Crap, two of those bloodsuckers got away."

Sam looked at the other two and said, "They didn't get away because we're going after them and their other bloodsucking friends. Reload those weapons, boys, and let's go kick ass."

Blood Fangs

SAMANTHA SAVAGE
BEAST HUNTRESS

CHAPTER 27

It Ends Right Here

IT ENDS RIGHT HERE

Duba and the other blood beast made their way back into the ship's galley where Delphine and the other blood beasts were feasting on the brother. Delphine looked up with blood on her face as Duba entered the galley. She asked, "I heard shots, but did you finish the humans off?"

Keeping his distance from Delphine, Duba replied, "No, my queen, it was a trap. They killed three of us." He paused for a second.

In a demanding tone, Delphine said, "Go on, what else?"

Duba replied, "The day walker was with them."

Delphine went into a rage. She flung the brother's body across the room. One of her fellow vampires tripped in front of her. She reached down and snapped his head off like it was a pretzel. Delphine threw the decapitated head at Duba, striking him in the chest and sending him into the next room. She screamed, "It ends right here, tonight!" She looked at Duba and said, "Gather all the clan to my chambers, and we'll have a surprise for our visitors." She looked around the room and screamed, "Go now!" In a second, Delphine was gone. The other blood beasts knew what needed to be done.

A few minutes later Sam, Portagee, and Big Mac made their way down to the lower deck. They slowly went through the rooms and cabins on the lower deck, expecting a trap. Finally, they came to the hatch door of the galley. Sam stood at the door and whispered, "Big Mac, when I fling this door open, you be ready to fire off that snake charmer if need be." Big Mac nodded his head in agreement.

Sam shoved open the hatch door and rolled head over heel in a tight ball into the galley. Big Mac was right behind her, holding out his snake charmer with both hands. Within seconds, it was evident that the blood beasts had been in the galley, but were nowhere to be found now.

Sam kicked a chair across the room and said, "Those bastards are up in the queen snake's chambers. I'm really not excited about going back up there again."

Portagee asked, "Why don't we just wait until dawn and set fire to this riverboat and watch it burn?"

Sam replied, "Good thought, but I want to make sure we kill the queen bitch. I can't be wondering if we got her or not. Yeah, we've got to go up there, and she'll be waiting for us."

As the trio was leaving the galley, Big Mac looked over at the corner and saw something that caught his attention. He waved his hand and said, "Hold on just a second." He went over to the dark corner and picked up something. Big Mac walked back over to Sam and Portagee and said, "Look, this snake charmer was Spike's. Those bastards are going to wish they had destroyed this pistol. I'm going to make them eat it." He flipped open the chamber to make sure it was fully loaded and then snapped it closed again. He looked at Sam as he cocked the hammers back on both snake charmers and said, "I'm going to shoot first and screw asking any questions. Then I'll shoot again."

Portagee and Big Mac slowly made their way up the outer deck stairs while Sam leaped from one level to the next. Dawn was not far away. The swamp had become eerily quiet. It almost seemed like the creatures of the swamp knew something was about to happen. Sam was waiting for the other two when they reached the top deck. Sam looked around and said, "My senses aren't picking up anything within fifty yards of the riverboat."

Portagee added, "Well, we all know where the party is then, Sam."

The three walked cautiously down the outer walkway and headed toward the entry hatch to Delphine's chamber. As they neared the hatch, Big Mac asked, "Do you want me to go in firing?"

Sam did not answer immediately; instead she kept walking. Once she got to the hatch door, she signaled Portagee to step forward. Then Sam whispered, "When I fling this door open, you throw in a flash grenade."

Portagee whispered back, "With great pleasure."

Sam unlatched the hatch and kicked it wide open. She looked at Portagee and yelled, "Do it!"

Portagee pulled the pin and threw the grenade into the chamber. Then she ducked back out of the way so as not to get blinded by the flash explosion. A few seconds went by and nothing happened. Sam looked down at Portagee and said, "It's a dud! Quick, throw another one."

Portagee stumbled around for a few seconds trying to pull another grenade from his pocket. Just as he threw another one into the room, two blood beasts flew through the hatch door. The flash explosion threw Portagee and Big Mac back on the deck. Portagee jumped back to his feet and quickly looked around, but Sam was gone. Next, he heard several splashes in the swamp below.

The blood beasts had each grabbed Sam by an arm and crashed off the upper deck to land in the swamp with her. As they hit the water, Sam swung her arms and cracked the two blood beasts together causing then to let go of her. As the three of them dog paddled in the water, Sam said, "What's the matter, boys, you had enough?"

One of the blood beasts looked at the other one and said, "Let's drown this bitch." The two leaped at Sam and took her under the water.

Sam's sonar senses had kicked in, and she knew that there was now a great movement in the swamp. She knew this was not going to be the place she wanted to be in a few minutes. Sam clawed at the two blood beasts, causing blood to flow in the swamp waters. The gators would pick this up quickly, and a feeding frenzy would surely follow. Sam's air supply was quickly running out. One blood beast had his arm wrapped around her neck while the other blood beast was wrapped around her legs. Sam was struggling to free herself from the blood beast that had a death grip around her neck. All of the sudden, she sensed a huge object swimming at a high speed directly at her head. With only seconds to react she flipped the blood beast that was wrapped around her neck to the front of her. Before the blood beast could do anything he was in the jaws of the huge gator. With several more gators closing in on her, she reached down, grabbed the head of the other blood beast, and snapped it off. With the murky swamp now filled with blood, Sam made a powerful downstroke with her arms and shot like a rocket toward the surface. Just as her head cleared the swamp waters, she found herself looking straight into the open jaws of a gator. Sam yelled out, "Oh crap!" Before the gator could clamp down on her, she reached up and grabbed the gator by his open jaws. Knowing that gators can exert thousands of pounds of clamping pressure with their jaws, Sam used all her energy to force the gator's jaws open wider. The gator went into a death roll with his jaws wide open. With one final push, Sam split the gators head in half as the two rolled over and over in the swamp. With more gators on the way, Sam leaped back onto the lower deck of the riverboat.

From the top deck, Portagee could now see that Sam was safe. He yelled down to her, "Sam, are you all right?"

Before he could say another word, he heard a thump right behind him. A voice behind him said, "Why in the bloody hell have you not gone into Delphine's chamber?"

Big Mac replied first. "I agree," he said. He turned and walked through the hatch with both snake charmers drawn. As he looked around the chamber, he saw several burnt images on the floor. Without looking behind him, he yelled out, "I think we got the bloodsucking bastards."

Sam and Portagee entered the chamber. Sam looked at the burnt spots on the floor and said, "This was too easy. Plus there should be many more dead blood beasts than this. Portagee, look around and use your detective skills. There must be a doorway or passage to another room."

Portagee looked around the chamber. Finally, his eyes fixed on a huge oil painting of Queen Delphine on the wall. He pointed at the painting and said, "There's your gateway to the undead. Just behind that painting is where you'll find them."

Blood Fangs

SAMANTHA SAVAGE
BEAST HUNTRESS

CHAPTER 28

Gateway to the Darkside

GATEWAY TO THE DARKSIDE

Portagee walked over to the painting, looking for a trip switch to reveal the passageway. After waiting for a few minutes, Sam was getting impatient. She walked over to the painting and said, "Portagee, step aside. I'm tired of waiting to find this bitch." She held her arms straight up in the air and said, "Let the cat claws solve this mystery." In a second, her fingernails grew out almost an inch. With her sharp nails, she ripped the painting to shreds in seconds.

Big Mac finally said, "You know, honey, that's an antique painting you just ripped to pieces."

Sam smiled and said, "Yeah, I know. Fitting for the queen, don't you think?" She finally stopped, reached into the void created where the painting had been ripped, and pulled on a trip wire. The painting moved sideways to reveal a passageway. After looking down the long dark passageway, Sam turned to Portagee and said, "Light up that passageway with another flash grenade. That will give those bloodsuckers something to think about."

Portagee replied, "That's not going to happen, Sam."

Sam looked puzzled by the answer. She asked, "Why not?"

Portagee added, "I used the last one coming through the hatch."

Sam snapped back, "Well hell, then we'll be guided by sonar senses and snake charmers."

Big Mac added, "What are you waiting for, girl?"

Sam knew the passageway couldn't be that long as the riverboat wasn't that big. After a short walk, the trio entered a dimly lit chamber. There were candles placed sparsely around the chamber, but that did little to help Portagee and Big Mac see much of anything. Sam could rely on her senses and could feel the movement around the room. As the trio stepped forward into the room, a sliding door slammed behind them blocking their exit. Sam could now sense that the walls all around them were moving, almost like snakes.

Portagee whispered, "Welcome to my web, said the spider to the fly."

Sam whispered back, "Big Mac, when I say 'fire', start firing in a circle until you run out of ammo. This place is crawling with blood beasts. Portagee, when he quits firing, start squirting holy water everywhere. Then maybe, Big Mac, you'll have a chance to reload." She paused for a second and then yelled out, "Fire!" As she yelled, she grabbed Portagee and pulled him to the floor with her.

Big Mac yelled out, "Fire in the hole, you bloodsuckers." He fired off round after round in all directions. The smoke from the snake charmers filled the chamber. Now no one could see anything. The screams from dying blood beasts and the firing of the snake charmers were almost ear shattering. A few seconds later, Big Mac had emptied his chambers of bullets.

While Big Mac attempted to reload, Portagee jumped up and began rapidly firing his holy water squirt gun. Based on the smell of burnt skin and continued screaming, Sam could tell they were killing blood beasts.

Big Mac managed only to reload one snake charmer before he was attacked from all sides. The other snake charmer went flying across the chamber. He shoved the snake charmer into the mouth of one of the blood beasts and ripped off a shot. He was still overwhelmed by the other blood beasts attacking him.

Sam left Portagee to fend for himself with his squirt gun and tried to intervene in Big Mac's struggle. Her adrenalin kicked in, and in a second, she reached her full power. She leaped on the back of one of the blood beasts that was biting and clawing at Big Mac. Sam yelled, "You just bit your last human!" She pulled him off Big Mac and turned him around at the same time. With a hard right thrust of her fist, she broke through the blood beast's rib cage and crushed his heart. He fell over in an instant.

With his arms free, Big Mac turned over and landed on top of another blood beast. He said, "I could just crush you right now with my weight, but I don't have the time." He moved the barrel of his snake charmer over the blood beast's chest and fired off a round through his heart.

Meanwhile, Sam picked up the last blood beast, raised him over her head, and snapped his back in two pieces. The screaming blood beast found himself back in front of Big Mac only to receive a shot through his heart.

The trio quickly tried to position itself for the next wave of attacks when out of nowhere a voice said, "Very impressive."

A moment later, several torches were lit. The torches illuminated the smoke-filled chamber with just enough light so that Sam could see their predicament. They were standing in the middle of the chamber, still surrounded by blood beasts, and Queen Delphine sat on a throne that appeared to be made out of human skulls and bones.

Portagee nudged Sam in the side and whispered, "Look what's above Delphine's throne. Sam looked and could not believe her eyes. Etched on the wall was an image of a triangle.

Sam whispered back, "That's exactly the same portal triangle symbol that's over the doorway at the Unfinished Cathedral in Bermuda. That's how they found their way into the Bermuda Triangle. There must be a portal behind the throne."

Big Mac interrupted by stepping forward, gently pushing Sam and Portagee aside. He pointed his snake charmer directly at Delphine. Delphine laughed and said, "You big oaf. From this distance, by the time you pull that trigger, I will be on you like flies on honey and slit your throat."

Sam took his arm and lowered it with her hand. In a low tone she said, "Bide your time, big man."

Delphine went on to say, "Wise decision to lower that weapon." She looked over at Sam and added, "Day walker, I thought I had turned you, but here you are—still an inferior human. You had your chance; now you and your friends will be our feast tonight." She snapped her fingers and iron bar window guards sealed off every window in the chamber. Delphine continued, "You're outnumbered five to one, so save us some time and drop your weapons."

While Delphine was talking, Big Mac was quietly reloading his snake charmer. Sam stepped forward and said, "Why don't you save us all some time, and you and I finish this off right now?"

Delphine smiled as she sat on her throne and replied, "You're not a challenge to me. Any one of my clan members can finish you off." She looked at Duba and said, "You can be my second. Destroy this bitch."

Duba bowed in front of Delphine and said, "I will gladly rip this day walker to shreds."

Sam turned to Portagee and Big Mac and said, "Watch my backside, mates." She turned back toward Duba as her eyes turned red to black and yelled, "I'm not a day walker, and you're going to get your ass kicked by a girl, you bloodsucker!"

Duba pulled out two machetes and began swinging them over his head. He extended his fangs, let out a scream, and charged at Sam. Sam waited until the last second and then leaped over his head. She landed behind him, and she quickly kicked his legs out from under him, sending him crashing to the floor. Duba laid there for a second, impaled on one of his own machetes. Sam knew the fight was not over.

Duba rolled over and stood up. He pulled the machete out from his midsection and licked the blade. He stared at Sam and said, "Next time, I'll be licking your blood off my blade."

Sam snapped back, "The hell you will." Duba quickly swung one of the machetes at her. Sam avoided the blade and grabbed his wrist. She snapped the bones in his wrist, ripped off his hand, and tossed it to the floor. Although Duba was in excruciating pain, he was still able to shove his other machete through Sam's backside. Sam dropped to her knees while Duba stumbled a few feet away.

Portagee started to run for Sam, but Delphine screamed out, "Little man, you move one more step and I swear it will be your last."

Still bent over in pain, Sam waved Portagee off and said, "Stay put; now's not the time. I'm all right." She stood up and turned back around with blood trickling from her mouth. Sam pulled the machete from her back and stumbled forward.

Queen Delphine stood up and clapped her hands. She looked at Duba and said, "Go ahead and finish this bitch off now. I'm getting thirsty seeing her blood."

Duba looked down at the bleeding stub where his hand once was and yelled, "Now I'm really pissed!" He leaped through the air screaming like a madman. He held his machete over his head like a pocket knife pointing at Sam. His sudden move was so fast all Sam could do was to stick her arms straight out. The impact of the collision was so horrific Sam crashed to the floor with Duba landing on top of her.

For what seem to be an eternity, both bodies appeared to be lifeless. Finally, there was a sign of movement, but no one in the chamber could tell who was moving. After seeing this, Delphine commanded, "Duba, bring me the day walker. It's time to feed."

A second later Duba rolled off of Sam and fell flat on his back. Sam was slowly trying to get up. Portagee and Big Mac moved quickly to help her get to her feet. Once on her feet, she said, "I don't thing Dumb Dumb is going to do anything with the machete that's stuck through his heart." Sam looked Delphine straight in the eyes and said, "Come on, Queen Bitch, now let's end this."

Delphine was enraged. She screamed out, "Kill them all now!" Instantly, the room full of blood beasts attacked the trio in overwhelming force. Portagee was firing off wooden stakes from his wrist blaster and firing off his holy water squirt gun in the other hand. Big Mac was bashing and throwing blood beasts in any direction he could.

It was evident to Sam that this final assault of the blood beasts was not survivable. She knew there was only one chance. She hoped she was right. She yelled to Big Mac, "Fire your snake charmer at the windows." No sooner had she said that than she was overpowered by blood beasts.

Big Mac quickly smashed the face in on a blood beast that was wrapped around him. This freed him to start firing at windows on both sides of the chamber. Every shot scored a hit and the chamber was instantly filled with deadly rays of sunlight. Sam's gamble had paid off; it was now dawn. The blood beasts were screaming from the agony of their bodies burning up. As the remaining blood beasts tried to kill them, Sam, Portagee, and Big Mac pulled the blood beasts into the sunlight, letting the morning rays slash through their bodies like laser beams. There was no place for the remaining blood beasts to run. They were all being incinerated by the flames and the sun's rays.

When the blood beasts all appeared to be dead, Portagee looked at Sam and said, "How the hell are we going to get out of here before this riverboat burns up?" Before Sam answered, she looked over at the throne where Delphine had been standing. The throne had been knocked over and Sam could see a small passageway emanating with green lightning bolts. Sam yelled out, "That's how the Queen Bitch has survived all these years. If things go bad, she escapes through a portal just like we have in Bermuda."

She was interrupted by Big Mac moaning on the floor. Portagee ran over to look at him and said, "Sam, he's bleeding badly. We need to get him out of here." Sam ran over to the steel door and pulled as hard as she could to slide it open. At first it wouldn't budge, but finally Sam managed to slide it open a couple of feet.

She looked at Portagee and said, "Get Big Mac out of here quickly. I can't hold this door open much longer."

Portagee yelled back as he helped Big Mac through the doorway, "I can't leave you here."

As Portagee passed her in the doorway, Sam reached into his backpack and pulled out something. As soon as he cleared the doorway Sam said, "Get off this boat before it explodes." Before Portagee could say anything else the door slammed shut, sealing Sam in the burning room.

Portagee turned and tried to pry open the door, but to no avail. He grabbed hold of Big Mac and helped him hobble out onto the open deck. The entire upper deck of the riverboat was now on fire, and the middle deck was almost consumed. The old riverboat was burning up like balsa wood. Finally, they made it down to the lower deck, but they still had a very big problem. Their air boat had been set loose to drift away by the blood beasts. Portagee looked around and by sheer luck he saw the air boat drifting about twenty yards away from the riverboat. He knew if he tried to swim that far he would end up as gator bait. Portagee looked up to see the old cargo crane burning, but still intact. He sat Big Mac down on the deck and said, "I'm going to play Tarzan and try to swing out to the boat. Wait here for me."

Big Mac laughed and said, "Little buddy, does it look like I'm going anywhere?"

Portagee reached up and grabbed the steel hook that was secured to the crane's rope. He backed up the burning stairs and leaped out as far as he could. In the middle of the swing, he yelled out, "Geronimo!" Halfway out to the air boat the burning rope snapped in two, sending Portagee in freefall to land in the swamp about five yards short of the boat.

Big Mac yelled out, "There's one hell of a big ass gator closing in on you fast."

Portagee started swimming for his life, but the gator was going to be on top of him in seconds. Portagee looked over his shoulder and all he could see was the wide open jaws and the long teeth about to clamp down on him. Portagee turned to try to protect himself from the gator when out of nowhere he heard, "Bang, bang, bang." The gator's jaws snapped closed just missing Portagee and slipped under the water.

Portagee looked up to see what had happened, only to see Big Mac pointing his faithful snake charmer at the gator. The gun barrel was still smoking. Big Mac yelled out, "That damn gator sank. How in the hell are we going to have that barbecue now?"

Still shaken, Portagee quickly climbed on the boat and raced over to pick up Big Mac. Within minutes, he had Big Mac off the burning riverboat, and they made their way about fifty yards away from the raging inferno.

Meanwhile, Sam knew she might still have one chance to escape. She was also not about to let Delphine escape again just to come back and begin another reign of terror. Sam ran over to the throne and kicked it out of the way. She said to herself, "I hope the bloody hell this is a portal gateway just like in Bermuda. Delphine must have some type of gateway key to open the portal. Oh bloody hell, here I go." In her hand, she lifted up the Tucker Cross that she had quickly taken out of Portagee's backpack as he left the chamber.

Sam aimed the Tucker Cross into the portal. Her newfound powers quickly ignited the cross. Green lights began emanating from the entrance while lightning started to strike deep within the portal.

Sam knew she was about out of time. The burning ceiling of the chamber was falling down all around her. Finally, the gateway opened with the green explosions going on throughout the portal. It was next to impossible for Sam to see through to the other side because of the smoke. Sam ran as fast as she could through the small portal. It was literally collapsing behind her as she ran. At the last second, she leaped into the green lightning as a huge explosion catapulted her through the gateway. Sam's body was in a freefall. In seconds, she had blacked out from the explosion.

Back on the air boat, Big Mac and Portagee were watching the burning riverboat in hopes that Sam would still escape. The explosion from the portal created a mega-explosion that blew the riverboat into a million pieces. The concussion blast from the riverboat knocked Portagee and Big Mac flat on their backs. By the time they sat up, there was nothing but burning debris floating on the water.

Portagee knew he had just lost his best friend. Big Mac tried to comfort him, but neither one of them could muster any words. Finally, Big Mac started up the air boat and began looking for a way out of the swamp. As Portagee sat staring out into the swamp, he noticed something about his backpack. It seemed way too light. He took off the backpack and began rummaging through it. After a few seconds he jumped up yelling, "Sam's alive, Sam's alive! I know it!"

Big Mac stopped the boat and said, "What the hell did you say?"

Excitedly, Portagee explained, "Sam took the cross from my backpack. She must have known it was a key to that portal behind Delphine's throne. That explosion that just happened must have been her going through the portal."

Big Mac scratched his head and said, "I don't know what the hell you said except that Sam is alive. I pray you're right."

Portagee replied, "I know I'm bloody right. Now we just have to wait for her to come back."

Big Mac asked, "How long will that be?"

Portagee hesitated to answer, but finally he said, "Last time it was eight months."

Big Mac replied, "Oh hell."

The two decided to go back to New Orleans and figure out what to do. It never occurred to either one of them that Sam might be blasting herself into a deadly trap.

SAMANTHA SAVAGE
BEAST HUNTRESS

CHAPTER 29

Beauty and the Beast

BEAUTY AND THE BEAST

When Sam woke up, she found herself in a very dark, damp room. She could hear the sound of dripping water. Either she was in a very dark cave or had been passed out for hours. As she got to her feet, she sent out her sonar senses like a bat would in a cave. She sensed movement several hundred yards away. She made her way slowly through the cave as she realized where she was. She was back in the Bermuda Triangle, and yes, she was in one of the Crystal Caverns. She knew that as she went farther, the crystals in the cave would light up her way. Sam felt that if she was quiet, she might have the element of surprise on Delphine. After all, Delphine probably thought she had made a clean getaway. Sam continued tracking Delphine's movements. After about an hour, her movement completely stopped. It dawned on Sam that it must still be daylight up on the surface. Delphine would have to wait it out until the sun set.

Sam was now within twenty yards of Delphine and sparkling crystals in the cave created a dim lighting effect. As Sam crept closer, a voice spoke out, "I've been waiting for you."

Sam knew she had been spotted. She stepped out from a rock formation in the cavern and said, "Yeah, I'm here to end your reign of terror."

Delphine stood up and faced Sam. She snapped back, "You're nothing but an inferior human trying to block my way to return to my beloved New Orleans."

Sam smiled and said, "I've got a news flash for you, bitch. I destroyed your portal and your riverboat when I passed through the gateway. So you're not going anywhere except to hell."

Delphine laughed, and immediately she transformed into a blood beast from hell. Her fangs and claws were much longer than any of the other blood beasts Sam had seen. Her body was now rippled with muscles. With her black piercing eyes, Delphine asked, "Are you sure you want a piece of this? Maybe you should just submit, and I'll let you die quickly."

Sam was shocked at the beast that was now standing in front of her. She had underestimated the powers of a blood beast hundreds of years old. Finally, she said, "Well, I guess it's going to be a battle of the beauty and the beast." Before Delphine could respond, Sam leaped into the air and grabbed a good size stalactite. She spun around on it and struck Delphine feet first in the back. Delphine went rolling across the floor and struck her head on a large rock. Sam said, "You know what they say, Delphine—the bigger they are, the harder they fall."

Delphine stood up and faced Sam. Her forehead had a large bleeding gash on it, but within seconds, the wound completely healed, leaving only the bloody residue on her forehead. Delphine smiled and yelled, "You little tramp! Did you really think you could hurt me?"

Sam knew if she pissed Delphine off more she might react without thinking clearly. So she obliged her and said, "Well duh! That was the idea, you stupid bitch."

Delphine was so angry now she leaped at Sam with her fangs protruding as far as they could. Sam had already felt her normal fangs, and there was no way in hell she was going to let those monster fangs stick into her neck. Sam misjudged Delphine's speed. She leaped high enough to cause Delphine to miss her neck, but she was not quick enough to totally get out of the way. Delphine's fangs ripped into one of Sam's inner thighs. Sam screamed out in sheer agony. Delphine clamped hold of Sam with a death grip and was not going to let go until she drained Sam of all her blood. In desperation, Sam was frantically feeling around the cave floor for some type of weapon before it was too late. Finally, she grabbed hold of a stalagmite that was about three feet long. She managed to snap it off at the base. With the snap of her wrist, she flipped it over so she could swing it like a club. Sam screamed out, "Let go, you bitch!" She bashed Delphine over the head with her club again and again until Delphine rolled away. Sam stood up as quickly as she could with blood squirting out of both fang gashes on her leg. Sam tried to hobble away as she ripped off her belt and applied it like a tourniquet to her thigh.

Delphine was now in a feeding frenzy. With Sam's blood running down her face, she charged Sam again with glazed-over, crazed eyes. Sam could not escape by running so she stood her ground. As Delphine reached out with her claws, Sam reached back to her past experiences growing up with a father who was a boxer. She hit Delphine with a roundhouse right fist in the jaw that stopped her dead in her tracks. Next, with a solid left uppercut to her chin Delphine crumpled and fell over backwards. The sudden shock to Delphine's system caused some of her powers to fade slightly. Sam could sense this. When Delphine tried to sit up, Sam dropped to one knee and hit her with another uppercut to the chin. As Delphine was falling backwards, Sam reached down and grabbed one of her protruding fangs and snapped it off. Delphine rolled over, screaming in pain.

Still holding the fang in her hand, Sam yelled, "Get up, you bloodsucker! You're not going to suck my blood or anyone else's again!" Delphine stood back up, slowly recovering her powers. She leaped at Sam, grabbing her long blonde hair and flipped her over her back. Luckily for Sam, she landed on her feet. She quickly spun Delphine around and grabbed her by her head.

At the same moment, she shoved both of her feet into Delphine's stomach and flipped her over her head. Both Sam and Delphine landed on their backs. Sam rolled over and looked up to see that Delphine had landed on a stalagmite. It was protruding up through her midsection. Her dark reddish-black blood was flowing everywhere.

Gasping for breath, Delphine exclaimed, "You fool! This won't kill me!"

Sam snapped back, "Yeah, but this will." She leaped high in the air on her good leg and kicked a stalactite on the ceiling of the cave. It fell directly over Delphine's heart, piercing her chest and splitting her heart in two. As Sam landed, she lunged down with her right hand and embedded Delphine's broken fang deep into her forehead. Sam collapsed flat on her back and said, "I think you're dead now, bitch." A minute later, Delphine's body self-ignited and was instantly engulfed in flames, soon disintegrating into a pile of ashes. Sam looked down at the ashes and saw a brilliant gold triangle medallion encrusted with seven green emeralds in it. She reached down and picked up the medallion by its gold chain. She knew this was another gateway key to the Bermuda Triangle.

Sam limped her way out of the cave. It was still in the predawn hours, which was fortunate for her. Her healing powers worked much better without the sun's rays. It was so good to smell the salty air of the Bermuda Triangle. To many people the Triangle was a prison, but to her it was a sanctuary. Sam knew she would have to leave the Bermuda Triangle soon on her quest to track down and destroy other blood beasts, but for now this would do. She found a small clearing not far from the cave entrance and lay down in a bed of sweet-smelling clover to relax. She quickly fell into a much needed sleep, knowing tomorrow would be another day in paradise.

MORE NOVELS BY
R.C. FARRINGTON

Blood Fangs
Quest for the Dark One

It was the year of our Lord, sixteen hundred and twenty-nine. For over one hundred years, Zuka, dark prince of the jungle, and his blood beasts, have ravaged the local native tribes deep within the Congo jungle.

Ambushed by one of the neighboring tribes, Zuka and his vampire clan are trapped and caged like animals, then rafted down the Congo River to an awaiting slave ship that will take them to the new world. After entering the unknown turbulent waters of the Bermuda Triangle, a horrific hurricane rips their ship to pieces and transports the few survivors into the parallel world of the Bermuda Triangle.

For hundreds of years, these vampires have plundered and killed the lost inhabitants in the Bermuda Triangle. Zuka and his clan of blood beasts are determined to find a portal back to the present-day world to avenge his betrayal and wreck havoc on an unsuspecting population as they search to find a dark queen.

This rare strain of blood beasts has very extraordinary powers that make them almost indestructible. There is no end to their thirst for blood.

After a ten-year absence from the Bermuda Triangle, the Spinners (from the Spinners Trilogy) are now young adults and must return to the Triangle to help their friends. They have to stop the blood beasts before they can find the gateway that allows them to return to the world they were banished from almost four hundred years ago.

The Spinners will only have one chance to stop these beasts. In this epic battle of man versus blood beast there can just be one survivor.

Awards:

"Blood Fangs—Quest for the Dark One" was awarded the Shreveport–Bossier regional 2012 Bronze ADDY award.

Phantom Marauders of the Bermuda Triangle

Drug lords who will stop at nothing to distribute their illegal drugs have law enforcement officials around the world outgunned, outnumbered, and sometimes outwitted. They have made a mockery out of the criminal justice system and are winning the war on drugs.

In response to this failure of law enforcement and the criminal-justice system, a desperate plan to eradicate drug trafficking has been conceived on the tiny island of Bermuda. With the aid of the United States, the island's Governor has declared war on the drug lords of South America and the Caribbean. By issuing a long-forgotten license to privateers to seek and destroy drug smugglers with no legal entanglements, the governor has leveled the playing field of the war on drugs. This Letter of Marque to privateers encompasses the waters of the Bermuda Triangle.

These marauders now have the license to attack and destroy drug trafficking enemies of the state. Although the Treaty of Paris of 1856 has long since banned privateering, the United States never signed the treaty. In fact, the United States Constitution still to this day permits Letters of Marque and Reprisal.

Turk Black, the captain of the ghost ship *The Phantom*, and his crew of Bermudians and Americans are hell-bent on wreaking havoc on drug trafficking in the Atlantic Ocean. Not since Blackbeard, with his ship *Queen Anne's Revenge,* has there been so much terror and destruction on the open seas.

With bounties on their heads and no safe ports to enter, *The Phantom* and her crew are marked by death squads of the drug cartels. Outnumbered one hundred to one, *The Phantom* and her crew play a deadly cat and mouse game using modern technology to evade, track, and destroy the drug traffickers. The tide is about to turn.

Awards:

"Phantom Marauders of the Bermuda Triangle" was awarded the Shreveport–Bossier regional 2012 Bronze ADDY award.

Death Diamonds of Bermudez

Modern-day Apartheid mercenaries from South Africa hell-bent on establishing an independent Boer Nation will stop at nothing to ignite their coup d'état. Finding the Death Diamonds is the final piece of the puzzle in their diabolical scheme.

A small group of renegade Boer War soldiers imprisoned in Bermuda in the early nineteen hundreds discovered the treasures of Bermúdez, but never revealed the location. With the most evil intentions, their descendants have searched for the Death Diamonds of the lost city of Bermúdez to this day.

Special FBI Agent Derrick Storm and Bermuda Inspector Ian Savage are the only ones who have any chance of keeping these ruthless mercenaries from fulfilling their diabolical scheme. Outgunned and outmanned, Savage and Storm must rely on their gut instincts to outwit these killers.

The Spinners (from the Spinners Trilogy) find themselves drawn into a treasure hunt cloaked with deceit and deception. Somehow Savage, Storm, and the Spinners must find the Death Diamonds first and prevent a nightmare of death and destruction.

Awards:

"Death Diamonds of Bermudez" was awarded the Shreveport– Bossier regional 2009 Silver ADDY award.

The Isle of Devils Holy War

The most explosive terrorist plot in history is about to become a reality.

A secret terrorist organization has used the Western world's greed for oil to cloak their Holy War. Undercover agents try to expose the terrorists' plot on the island of Bermuda before thousands of innocent lives are in jeopardy.

FBI agent Derrick Storm from the United States, with the assistance of Ian Savage, a police inspector from Bermuda, attempt to uncover the most sophisticated and deadly terrorist plot ever set in motion. FBI Agent Storm is one of the top law enforcement specialists in the United States. He has a great respect for the law but will bend the rules if necessary to apprehend criminals.

Inspector Savage has a "school of hard knocks" law enforcement degree. By Bermuda police standards, his actions are often unorthodox. In spite of that, he's one of the most effective crime fighters in Bermuda.

Somehow these two agents from different races, backgrounds, and countries must work together to derail a terrorist plot that grows into a serious threat to the security of the world.

Awards:

"The Isle of Devil's Holy War" was awarded the Shreveport– Bossier regional 2008 Gold ADDY award.

Spinners The Lost Treasure of Bermuda—Episode I

In Episode I, five teenagers unlock the secrets of the Bermuda Triangle where the past and the present collide. "The Lost Treasure of Bermuda" has intrigued and eluded treasure hunters for more than two hundred years. The Spinners have to face and survive evil villains in Bermuda and in the Bermuda Triangle who will stop at nothing to control the "Tucker Cross" and "The Lost Treasure."

Spinners The Protectors of the Bermuda Triangle—Episode II

Five teenagers from Bermuda are trapped in the Bermuda Triangle. They must face the forces of evil to protect the Triangle from destruction. Scarzo, a modern day mercenary from Brazil, kidnaps the Spinners, determined to force them to reveal the secret gateway to the Bermuda Triangle. The Spinners also have the bad fortune of crossing paths with Scorpion, a Voodoo pirate from Haiti. She will stop at nothing to find the power source that controls the Bermuda Triangle.

Spinners The Curse of the Bermuda Abyss—Episode III

Five teenagers trapped in the Bermuda Triangle find themselves being drawn into the dark depths of the Bermuda Abyss. In this third episode, the Spinners may have finally met their match as they face the most vicious and most notorious evil being of all time. In a race for their lives and with very little time, the Spinners must escape from the depths of the Bermuda Abyss and its curse.

www.ingramcontent.com/pod-product-compliance
Lightning Source LLC
Chambersburg PA
CBHW051455170626
46811CB00002B/498